THE RAG BAG FAMILY

He stood up and carried Adam over to a crib in the window bay. Gently, he settled him down. 'Well, that's my bit done,' he said. 'I'm afraid I've got to get off to work now, Rita, so I'll say goodbye. I won't see you until tomorrow, but I hope you settle in OK. It's really good to have you with us.'

'How do you know?' asked Rita suddenly.

'Know what?' asked Pete, surprised.

'How do you know it's good to have me? You don't know who I am. I might be the axe-murderer's daughter, for all you know. I might be planning to wait until you're asleep, and then creep into your room and plunge a chopper into your skulls.'

Also by Yvonne Coppard

Copper's Kid
Bully
Hide and Seek
Simple Simon

THE RAG BAG FAMILY

Yvonne Coppard

RED FOX

A Red Fox Book

Published by Random House Children's Books
20 Vauxhall Bridge Road, London SW1V 2SA

A division of Random House UK Ltd

London Melbourne Sydney Auckland
Johannesburg and agencies throughout the world

© Yvonne Coppard 1992

First published by The Bodley Head Children's Books 1992
Red Fox edition 1994

1 3 5 7 9 10 8 6 4 2

Printed and bound in Great Britain by
Cox & Wyman Ltd, Reading, Berkshire

RANDOM HOUSE UK Limited Reg. No. 954009

ISBN 0 09 926621 0

1

'Here we are then.' The bright red car drew smoothly alongside the curb. Rita looked at her new home without interest. It was a tall, narrow house, sandwiched into a scruffy terrace. In a small court-yard, a tree struggled to grow big and strong in the city air; it looked half-choked.

Like me, thought Rita suddenly. She felt the first pang of fear since she had watched her grand-mother, the only family she had left, lying in hos-pital.

'I don't want this,' she said. 'You know, I'd rather go to a children's home than this.'

Wendy Carfield sighed. It had been a long, hot day. As Rita's social worker, she had tried and tried to get Rita to talk about what was happening, without success. The child had refused point-blank to offer any opinion about where she should go while her gran was in hospital (Wendy had a feeling Rita knew there was a chance the old lady might never come home) or offer any clue about her fears for the future. She had not even asked whether they would trace her mother.

Foster families willing to take teenagers were very hard to find. Wendy had made dozens of calls, pleaded and persuaded and coaxed and perhaps even bullied her way to a place for Rita with a couple who could really help her through a very difficult time. Now they were here, and Rita was finally expressing an opinion. One phone call might have found a place in a children's home.

'I'm sorry, Rita,' she said gently. 'You may feel I didn't try hard enough to find out what you really wanted. But you wouldn't talk to me, and we had to move quickly. I know it's all been a terrible shock for you. . . . '

Rita hung her head, letting the long dark hair fall across her face. She wasn't going to talk about that.

Wendy put her hand on Rita's shoulder, and felt it stiffen. She patted Rita gently. 'Give it a chance, love, eh? Give the Browns a chance. If it really doesn't work out, well, we can talk again. Come on.'

Wendy wound up her window, got out of the car and locked the driver's door. She walked around to Rita's side. The child hadn't moved, and Wendy felt a surge of anxiety. The Browns had been reluctant to take another child, and she had played on their generous hearts to get Rita a place in their family. She didn't want to start with a scene. If Rita refused to get out of the car, she didn't know what she could do.

As Wendy stood, undecided, on the pavement, the front door of the house opened. A plump, smiling toddler waddled into the courtyard dressed only in a large terry nappy, which was beginning to slide. The toddler's hand was held by a small, dark woman with her hair clipped back in a red bow.

2

Both the child and the woman were smiling as they approached the car.

Rita, looking sideways at them through the dark net of hair which was beginning to make her face sweat in the hot sun, decided the woman must be the foster mother, Mrs Brown. She couldn't remember her first name. Wendy had told her, but Rita had not been listening to the details. She had trouble taking anything in at the moment. Wendy had seemed to know this without being told, and had kept telling her there was no need to remember everything, she could always ask questions.

'Hello, Rita,' said the woman, through the open window of the car. 'We saw you pull up, and Charlie here was too excited to wait for you to get to the door. He's been at the window all morning.'

As if to prove the point, the toddler put his plump hands on the window seal and tried clumsily to open the door. 'Tum on,' he said, 'tum on. Me want see you.'

Rita lifted her head, and Wendy held her breath.

Then 'Mind your fingers,' said Rita to the child, and she wound up the window, opened the door and got out.

Charlie immediately grabbed her by the thumb and pulled her towards the house. His nappy gave up the ghost and slid to the ground. He looked down briefly and with the ease of one for whom this was a very common occurrence, simply stepped out of it and left it lying on the pavement. Stark-naked, he continued to pull on Rita's hand.

'Sorry,' said the foster mother. 'I ran out of disposables, and these other ones need superglue to keep them on. We didn't really mean to welcome you to the family with a little flasher.'

'It's all right.' Rita smiled, and allowed Charlie to pull her towards the house. Wendy and the mother exchanged relieved glances and followed them in.

Rita had lived all her life in a one-bedroomed flat. With only two of them, there had been room enough. Gran had always gone for sober colours: dark-green curtains, brown-patterned carpet, a heavy wallpaper. What greeted her now was a complete contrast. The walls were bright sunshine yellow, the curtains vivid swirls of yellow and white. The ceilings were high, and the room was large. It felt light, and cheerful, and bustling. An enormous multi-coloured sofa along one side of the room was part-occupied by a man holding a baby and a bottle, a white-haired woman, and several cuddly toys. The foster mother went to sit beside the man and beckoned Wendy and Rita to the other sofa, a more sober-looking blue studio couch. And so they sat, opposite each other, like opposing teams. On the coloured sofa, the Brown family, and in the blue corner, the Social Worker and the Displaced Child. There had been times when such a thought would have made Rita smile.

Charlie waddled off to a corner of the room where a mesh playpen was piled high with assorted toys. He chose one for each hand and came back to Rita, depositing them in her lap with a smile. She smiled back. 'Thank you.'

'Come on, Charlie me lad,' said the older woman on the coloured sofa. 'Let's get you a clean nappy and tart you up a bit, eh?' She picked Charlie up, placing him on her hip, and turned to Rita. 'I'm

4

Annie's mum,' she said. 'You'll see a fair bit of me, I expect. I'm right sorry to hear about your gran, but I hope you'll be very happy here. You're certainly welcome, isn't she, Charlie?' She smiled indulgently at the toddler, who didn't understand a word but grinned back happily enough. He meshed his sticky fingers in her hair and waved as he was carried from the room.

Rita sat on the edge of the sofa. Her back was beginning to ache from being held so stiffly, and her head buzzed a bit too. If only she could curl up on the armchair in her own sitting room, with something good on the telly and Gran snoring in the background, then she could relax and be herself. But the person sitting in this big room with a lot of strangers must be someone else; she couldn't speak, and she couldn't move without an effort. The proper Rita was always chatting, always on the go. This new one who had taken over her body only wanted to do two things: run or sleep. She looked briefly across at the couple with the baby, who were smiling nervously at her, and then swung her face behind her hair again.

'I'm sorry this has all been done in a rush,' said Wendy. Rita didn't know if she was talking to the Browns or to her; perhaps all three. 'Naturally we'd have liked more warning that Rita was coming into care, and then we could have planned things properly. I've explained to Rita as much as I can about what's happening, and about the set-up here. But I'm sure we all know how hard it must be for her, being chucked in at the deep end without introductory visits and so on.'

'Yes, it must be awful,' said the foster mother. 'I

5

wonder, Rita, how much you remember of what Wendy has told you about us. It must be hard to take in new information when your mind is already taken up with worrying about your gran.'

Rita looked up, surprised. This woman had put into words exactly what Rita was feeling. She couldn't even remember how many people there were in this new family, still less their names.

'I'm Annie,' said the woman, 'and this is my husband Pete.'

Pete, a tall man with very short, curly hair and a face which reminded Rita of the Robin Hood in an old film she had seen, smiled. 'Hi.' He was rubbing the baby's back; the baby burped and dribbled. Annie leaned over to wipe his mouth and chin with his bib.

'Pete's the strong, silent type,' grinned Annie. 'He doesn't say much, but he's good at listening. And there in his arms is Adam. He's four months old, and he sleeps a lot. He's been with us since he was only five days, and he'll be leaving soon because he's going to be adopted. We will miss him like mad.'

Rita wanted to ask why his mother wasn't keeping him, or why the Browns weren't adopting him if they would miss him so much, but she didn't dare. Instead she said, 'Poor baby.'

'I think he'll be all right,' said Annie gently. 'His own mum and dad couldn't take care of him, but he will be loved just as much by his new family. He'll grow up healthy and happy and strong, you'll see.'

But he'll wonder, thought Rita, just like I do. He'll wonder how his mother could have dumped him and left, as though he were nothing more than an unwanted Christmas present. He'll never be *quite* sure where he fits in. And at least I was dumped on my own gran, not complete strangers.

She said none of this, of course, just watched the baby lying peacefully in Pete's arms. Annie had paused, allowing Rita time to digest the information she had given. Now she carried on.

'You've met Charlie. He's nearly two, but very big for his age. I'm not sure how long he'll be here . . .'

'Isn't he . . . ? I mean, I thought he was yours,' said Rita. It hadn't occurred to her that Charlie could be a foster child. He fitted in so perfectly. Even the way Annie's mum had picked him up had been so natural, so perfectly what a grandmother would do with her own grandson, that Rita believed he was a 'proper child', a real member of the family and not just temporarily added on, like the baby and herself.

'No, he's not ours,' smiled Annie. 'Sometimes I wish he was, but he has a mum and dad who love him. His mum comes to see him a couple of times a week, but she isn't very well and can't look after Charlie properly at the moment.'

'Where's his dad?' asked Rita.

'Unfortunately, his dad's in prison,' said Annie. 'So Charlie doesn't see him at all, apart from a short visit when the journey can be arranged – the prison's in Staffordshire and it takes hours to get there.'

More unanswered questions crowded into Rita's mind. Why in prison? Why would Annie and Pete take a criminal's child? Rita's gran would have been shocked and dismayed.

'You've met my mother, too,' said Annie. 'Her name's Rosie, and she and my dad live just round the corner. Mum comes in almost every day to give me a hand with the housework and the babies and so on. I couldn't manage without her. You'll like her, Rita, she's very easy to get along with, isn't she Pete?'

'She's my mother-in-law. Would I dare say anything else?' laughed Pete. He looked down at the baby, Adam, who had fallen asleep in his arms. 'Are you off at last, young fella? It's time to hand you over anyway.'

He stood up and carried Adam over to a crib in the window bay. Gently, he settled him down. 'Well, that's my bit done,' he said. 'I'm afraid I've got to get off to work now, Rita, so I'll say goodbye. I won't see you until tomorrow, but I hope you settle in OK. It's really good to have you with us.'

'How do you know?' asked Rita suddenly.

'Know what?' asked Pete, surprised.

'How do you know it's good to have me? You don't know who I am. I might be the axe-murderer's daughter, for all you know. I might be planning to wait until you're asleep, and then creep into your room and plunge a chopper into your skulls.'

The expression on Wendy's face made Rita feel a whole lot better. Her smile hovered over her lips with a desperate air of determination.

'I . . . um . . . Rita . . .' murmured Wendy uneasily. She was completely floored.

Annie and Pete were not such easy targets. 'I can

8

see you have a flair for the dramatic,' said Annie with a smile.

Pete laughed aloud. 'You're right, Rita,' he said. 'We don't know you. For all we know, you could be planning to murder us in our beds and take the family silver. *But*, I trust Charlie. The boy has sound instincts. If Charlie thinks you're all right, that's enough for me. See you tomorrow, Rita. 'Bye, love.' He leaned over and kissed his wife. 'I'll ask your mum to make a cup of tea for you all, shall I?'

Annie nodded. 'Yes. Thanks. See you in the morning.'

Rita felt she had been put in her place. She had wanted them to know that she could stand up for herself, and she didn't know whether she was glad that they had not responded to her challenge, or angry. Where was Pete going, anyway? What kind of job did he have that meant being away from home at night? No-one had told her anything about this family that she could remember. The whole thing was a mess.

'Pete's a staff nurse,' said Annie, again seeming to read her thoughts. 'He's on nights at the moment, on the surgical ward. He doesn't start until seven but he's in charge, so he likes to get there early and chat to the patients. He eats with friends at the hospital canteen – but there's no need to worry. I don't think he does it to escape my cooking.' She laughed, but Rita's face had set into what Gran called her 'frozen look' and she couldn't thaw it.

'Where did I get to?' said Annie. 'I'm trying to tell you only the bare facts at the moment, because there's such a lot to take in. But if you've got questions, just ask them. Can you remember who we are so far?'

'Annie and Pete, Adam and Charlie, your mother Rosie,' repeated Rita. Did the woman think she was thick?

'Good. We're more than halfway now.'

Rita's heart sank. There were even more of them. She could just about cope with three new strangers, and the little ones didn't really count. Charlie was quite cute, actually. But this house was beginning to feel a bit like Piccadily Circus on a busy afternoon. How many more inquisitive eyes and questions was she going to be subjected to before this was all over?

'There are just three more to go,' said Annie kindly. 'That's Mark, who's sixteen, and Jody – she's fourteen, only a bit older than you, so you'll have someone to show you round and about. And finally there's Jason. He's nearly eight. They're all out with the dog at the moment. We didn't want to swamp you with the whole family at once. We're quite a crowd. Did you know we had a dog?'

Rita shook her head. Wendy was speaking, and she and Annie laughed together, but Rita heard the words only as a vague sound and didn't understand what they were saying. The urge to run was washed away by a longing to climb into bed – she no longer cared whether it was her own or a strange one – and pull the covers over her head. Maybe if she slept for long enough it would all be over when she woke up. She'd be back in the flat, with Gran moaning about her leaving cups in their bedroom and frying up bacon for breakfast. There'd be news on the radio and the clang of fire doors in the corridor outside the flat, and three days of freedom before the holidays ended and she had to go back to school.

But that wasn't going to happen. It had ceased to be a possibility yesterday morning, when Gran slid from her chair at breakfast time and stared at Rita as if she had no idea who she was. Her face, turned in amazement to her granddaughter, was lopsided and dribble came out of her mouth. The whole right side of her body looked odd, and she couldn't move it.

Rita had screamed, rushed to her gran's side. 'What's wrong, Gran? What's wrong?' And Gran hadn't answered, just made terrible growling sounds. Mrs Beavis next door had answered Rita's frantic knocking and taken charge. Now Gran lay miles away in a stiff white bed that she would hate if she knew what was happening and Rita was here, with strangers. They were apart for the first time in Rita's whole life, and Rita knew that however nice this family was to her, it wouldn't work out. From now, for the rest of her life, Rita Dennison was going to be a misfit. It was Gran's word for anyone who didn't have a clear place in her idea of what life should be about. Gran was not a tolerant woman, and there were many people she deemed to be misfits.

Fitting in was being with your own kin, in your own home, and knowing what you would be doing two, five, twenty years ahead. Rita's proper place and time had been decided long ago. She could never be happy anywhere else on earth than in her grandmother's flat, going to the local school until it was time to leave and get a job, then getting a job until it was time to bring up her own children. Now this had been snatched away. She had no idea what would happen next. Overnight, she had become a misfit. That's why she was here, in a family which never stayed the same, and had no sense of place. It seemed to be a family of people who were just passing through.

'Rita? Are you OK, love?' Wendy was peering through the mass of hair which Rita automatically used to shield herself when she thought there was a danger of crying. Rita nodded fiercely, and steeled herself for the next onslaught of kindness from strangers.

2

Rosie brought a tray of tea, with juice in a feeder cup for Charlie. He sat in the highchair beaming at everyone and occasionally bashing his cup on the tray in front of him. Charlie was oblivious to the tension in the room around him, but Rita felt it like a smothering blanket. She knew it was up to her. They were waiting for her to say something. Rita cast about for something cheery or witty, but found nothing in her brain except cotton-wool deadness.

'Um . . . how do you all fit in one house?' she asked. It sounded rude, and prying, and she wished she'd kept quiet.

But Annie smiled. 'I'll show you,' she said. 'Come this way for a guided tour of the mad-house.'

Annie led her into the hall and up the stairs – almost as many stairs as there were from the communal garden outside the block of flats to her own front door, but this time they were in the same house. The Browns must have pots of money. Was that why they fostered kids? How much did they charge? More questions she would never ask. Finally they reached the top. Rita had counted four floors, including the ground floor, and a little landing leading to some sort of extension. The place was massive.

They were in another sitting room. This one had yet another sofa, and some very big cushions on the floor. There was a table with a couple of chairs and a stack of games piled on to it. In the corner was a large colour television and video. 'Family room,' said Annie. 'Usually in a mess, but not too bad today. I've cleaned up especially for you!' she laughed. 'We don't have a television downstairs. I'm afraid you have to bargain with the others for the programmes you want to watch. Mark has a little set in his room, so it's not usually too bad.'

The house had two rooms on each floor, Rita discovered: one large and one smaller. Mark had the room at the top, next to the family room. Rita peeped in as they passed and discovered at once that he was a football fan; there were pictures and charts all over the wall. On the next floor down, the small room belonged to Jason and the large room was to be Rita's, shared with Jody. It had obviously been thoroughly cleaned that morning, and stood ready for its new occupant. The room had two windows, with a bed under each. It was easy to see which one was Rita's – the other bed had a nightdress across the bottom and two large rag dolls arranged carefully against the pillows. Rita's bed was the bare one. On one side of the room there were shelves. Some had been emptied, presumably for Rita's arrival. There were also two old-fashioned dressing tables and two wardrobes. On one dressing table there was an array of make-up, brushes, pots spilling over with cotton wool, beads, pads of paper. The other dressing table was completely bare.

The room was waiting for Rita's personal stamp, her own little bits and pieces which would proclaim that she had moved in. Rita's bed, Rita's dressing table, shelves, wardrobe. She and Gran had shared a wardrobe and a dressing table, and used the window sill for shelving. This was luxurious by comparison.

'It's very nice,' she said politely.

'You can put up posters if you want to,' said Annie. 'I think Jody has some sort of system – you know two walls for her, two walls for . . . '

' . . . whoever happens to be passing through,' Rita finished.

Annie blushed. 'I hope you're more than just a passer-through, Rita. But yes, I suppose you could put it that way.'

'Jody's your own child, then, is she?' asked Rita. It was the first time she had felt any genuine interest. It must be awful to have to share everything, even your mum and dad, with strangers. She wondered how Jody coped, and how much she minded.

'Yes, Jody's ours. That's to say, we adopted her when she was very tiny. Mark, too.'

'Adopted?' Rita framed a question, but decided it would be rude to ask it. 'What about the other one – the younger one?' Rita struggled unsuccessfully to remember his name. Such a lot of names.

'Jason,' supplied Annie. 'Jason has only been here three weeks – they're looking for a family who can take him permanently.'

So Jason wasn't theirs either. They had no

children of their own. Gran would have sniffed, and said they were mad to take on bairns when they had no need to. She herself had found one child more than enough, and it had only ever brought her sorrow, as she often pointed out. Rita sometimes wondered whether she included Rita as part of the sorrow that Kathleen, Rita's mother, had brought. Gran did not go in for cuddles and expressions of affection, but that was just her way.

They were climbing downstairs again. A half-landing led off to what seemed to be an extension to the house. 'Bathroom and loo,' said Annie. 'There's also a shower room – it's a bit cramped but we squeezed it in to lessen the waiting time in the mornings. My advice to you is to get in before Mark if you want the shower or the bathroom – whichever one *he* chooses, it'll be tied up for the best part of an hour. There's another shower and loo downstairs, near the garden door. I'll show you when we get there.'

The Browns' bedroom seemed to be swathed in tapestries and wall-hangings, like something from an Eastern bazaar in a picture book. Adam slept here too; there was a crib in the corner. Rita was intrigued, although she didn't want to go right into the room, not knowing if that would be good manners. The thing to do seemed to be to peep round the door, just to cement in her mind where all the rooms were and what their use was. Next to the Browns was a bright, cheery little bedroom. Rita saw a cot – obviously Charlie's. A flurry of hanging mobiles fluttered in a sudden breeze from the open window. There were toys all over the place. 'We'll

16

have to teach Charlie to clean up after himself,' laughed Annie.

The tour of the house finished with the dining room, dominated by a huge wooden table with eight place mats on it, and the kitchen, which had been built on to the back of the house. There was also a little room with a washing machine and tumble drier in it, and two clothes horses festooned with nappies.

'Well, that's it,' said Annie after she had shown Rita past the downstairs loo and shower into the small town garden. 'What do you think? Will it be OK?'

Rita looked around at the little lawn, the bright flowers drooping their heads in the summer sun, the garden loungers waiting for lazy occupants. It was like a house from a storybook. The perfect home for the perfect family. And yet really, it was a ragbag of problems – other people's problems which the Browns had gathered together like a couple of hens with no chicks of their own.

'Do you have a map I can borrow?' she asked, and attempted a smile. 'I think I'll get lost.'

Annie grinned. 'I'd better make a start on dinner. The others will be back soon – I told them to stay out as long as they could, to give you a chance to absorb one bit of us at a time, but their bellies will be rumbling by now. Do you like pizza?' Rita nodded. Annie turned to Wendy. 'How about you? Do you want to stay and have something with us?'

'That would be lovely, but no thanks,' said Wendy. 'As a matter of fact, I had better push off now – heavy date tonight.' She smiled.

Rita felt a sudden surge of panic, like a small

child suddenly finding itself lost in a busy shop. She had only met Wendy the previous day, at the hospital, but it was Wendy who had found out about Gran's condition and told her what the doctors said, Wendy who had arranged for her to stay near Gran on the ward all night. Wendy was the nearest thing Rita had to someone who knew her, and now she was running off and leaving her in this cavernous house full of strange people. She wanted to say, 'Take me with you. I'll stay out of the way, if you just let me come with you.' But that would be silly. There was no way out of what was happening, and Rita wasn't going to let them see she cared about that. So she muttered ''Bye then,' and turned away.

'I'll drop in tomorrow, and see how it's going,' said Wendy. 'I'll take you to see your gran, too. About four o'clock, OK?'

Rita shrugged. The mention of Gran made her want to cry. Wendy patted her shoulder and left, with a cheery wave. As Rita stood in the garden, wondering what to do next, there was a commotion in the hall. It sounded like the January sales two minutes after opening time, when hundreds of people were pushing through the doorway. From somewhere upstairs Charlie yelled, 'Tum in, tum in!'

Annie smiled. 'Ah, the returning hordes. It must be near feeding time. Come and meet the rest of the family, Rita.' She put her arm lightly round Rita's shoulder, not seeming to notice the stiffness of Rita's body.

As they reached the hall Rita had a shock. There was a dog waiting to greet her – a *huge* St Bernard

18

dog, with great jaws hanging open. It moved towards her, and she stepped back.

'It's all right,' said a voice. 'He's very gentle, aren't you, boy?'

A tall blond boy with light blue eyes and a wide smile appeared. 'This is Gnasher,' he said. 'We call him that because it's so far from the truth it's a joke. He might lick you to death, but he'd never hurt you.'

Rita stretched out her hand and Gnasher ambled up to her, his great head nuzzling against her waist. 'Watch out,' said the boy, whom she supposed must be Mark. 'He's very hairy, and he slobbers too. You have to wear washable clothes to be Gnasher's friend.'

Sure enough, when Rita looked down her jeans and shirt were covered in rust-brown hair and there were two wet patches where Gnasher had pushed his head against her. 'Yuk,' she said.

'You get used to it,' said the boy. 'When's dinner, Mum?'

'Soon. Where are Jason and Jody?'

'Jason dashed off upstairs – I think he's hiding all the bits of stick and stone he brought back from the woods before you have a chance to throw them away! Don't know where Jody is – she was here a minute ago.'

'I'm here,' came a voice from the dining room.

'Well come and say hello,' called Annie. There was a pause, and then Jody appeared in the dining room doorway, leaning against the frame.

She was beautiful. Rita felt instantly gawky, like the ugly duckling looking at the swan, except without the hope of ever becoming one.

Jody was a bit taller than Rita but slimmer. She had red-blonde hair which seemed to shimmer around her face. Her eyes were large and a curious green; they looked Rita over coolly, as if trying to assess whether she would be worth the bother of getting to know.

She wore jeans and a cotton T-shirt, just as Rita did, but there was a world of difference between them. Jody wore her clothes as if they were a part of her; she looked like a magazine advertisement. Rita felt very aware of the dark straight hair that needed a wash, and the spots forming on her chin. She felt the need to run coming back, and gritted her teeth. This made her look even worse, but better that than giving in to the impulse and flying down the street in a strange part of town. They'd have to chase her, bring her back, and that would be even more humiliating than this cool green-eyed girl looking her over as though she were in a market.

'Hello,' said Jody, and turned back into the dining room. Rita had not measured up to standard. She looked at Annie and saw that she was annoyed with Jody. As she caught Rita's eye, she smiled sheepishly. 'Jody can be a bit brusque,' she said, 'but I'm sure you'll get on all right. Look, can you go and find my mum? I think she's upstairs changing Adam. Ask her to bring the babies down and I'll see to their baths after dinner. She'll be wanting to get back home, I expect.'

Annie seemed to accept Rita as one of the family already, with an easiness that was hard to resist. 'Yes, OK,' said Rita. She saw, as she climbed the stairs, that Annie was heading for the dining room. She heard the door close firmly. Annie was going to have words with Jody. About me, thought Rita with a grim smile, about being kind to the poor little orphan off the streets, or else.

Of course, Rita was not actually an orphan. She had a mother somewhere, whose name was Kathleen. Rita had never seen a picture of her, not even in Gran's handbag where she had looked purposely, but she knew Kathleen was beautiful. Rita also had a father, probably still living, although she didn't know his name. So her roots were perhaps even better than Jody's, who had been adopted as a baby.

Gran would never have contemplated adoption. They had watched a programme once about women who had babies to give to other people who couldn't have any. Rita had thought this a good idea, but Gran had been outraged. 'Babies have places, just like everybody,' she had said. 'And a baby's place is with its own family, its own kith and kin.' That was why Kathleen, who didn't agree with her mother on this or on anything else, had left her baby in Gran's living room one day with a carrier bag full of nappies and clothes and then disappeared.

Rita wondered what Jody knew about her proper family. Probably nothing, so she had no right to get snooty with Rita.

'Finding your way about all right?'

Rosie's voice cut into the mist which seemed to surround Rita now whenever she thought about Gran, and she realized she was standing in the doorway of the babies' room, staring at Rosie who was just buttoning Adam's Babygro. Charlie was on the floor with his building bricks. 'Tum in, tum in!' he squealed delightedly.

'Sorry? Um, yes, think so. Um, Mrs Brown – Annie – asked me to tell you to bring the little ones down now. She'll bath them later.'

'I've done Adam already,' she said. 'But Charlie likes to splash about for a long time with his ducks, don't you my love?'

Charlie looked up from his bricks and smiled. 'Barf?'

'After dinner, Charlie. Dinner time now, then Mummy Annie will bath you.'

Mummy Annie. Rita hoped she wouldn't have to say that. From downstairs came the sound of raised voices – she couldn't tell whose – and then Annie's voice, sharp and insistent.

'There's a lot of 'em, isn't there?' said Rosie sympathetically. 'I can't keep track myself, sometimes.' She picked Adam up. 'Have you met the others?'

'Yes.' Rita pictured Jody's beautiful, slightly scornful face and sighed.

'Here.' Rosie held baby Adam out to her.

'Oh I couldn't – I've never held a baby. I might drop him!'

'Then again, you might not,' said Rosie firmly. 'Hold out your arms.' She moved Rita's arm into a cradle for the baby. 'Put your hand behind his head, and bring this arm up – there, you're doing fine.'

Rita looked at Adam, who stared up at her with a faintly quizzical expression. Who are you? he seemed to ask. I'm the new one, she answered silently. Another rag for the rag bag. The baby opened his mouth into a perfect little circle. Oh, he seemed to say. There was a small blister on his bottom lip, milk-coloured. He smelt lovely. 'He's beautiful,' whispered Rita.

'And so are you, chick. You're a natural with babies, you are.' She nodded at the baby. 'Young Adam there, he's already on his second mum, likely to have a third. But he's going to be all right in the end – and so are you.'

'Am I?' Rita looked up, straight into Rosie's eyes. 'How do you know?'

'How do I know? I just do. In this house, if things aren't going right, we find a way to *make* them go right. Count on it.'

Rita was very embarrassed at this 'smushy talk' as Gran would call it. But it was good to feel welcome, at least by some members of the family. Jody, she had a feeling, was not going to give her much joy as a room-mate.

Gran would tell her not to give in to despair. 'Stick out your chin and get on with it,' – Rita could almost hear Gran's voice. But it was only her imagination. Gran was silent, fighting for life in a strange hospital bed while Rita struggled in the wilderness without her.

3

'Well, how are things going?' asked Wendy the next day.

'Things?' Rita knew perfectly well what Wendy meant, but she was playing for time while she thought of something to say. It made her so weary, this constant pressure to share her life with other people. Are you all right? Is this OK? What are you thinking/feeling/doing? It was like being in a zoo. Wendy, the doctor looking after Gran, the foster parents – all of them watching her, being kind and understanding, asking questions she didn't want to answer but felt unable to refuse. After all, they were only trying to help. But Gran had never asked Rita about her innermost thoughts, and had often told her that the world was not interested in miserable people; problems were best kept to yourself. It wasn't that Gran wouldn't help, if asked. She had gone down to the school to sort out the French teacher who had given Rita an unfair detention, and she had put to flight the two boys in the park who had trapped Rita on the slide and refused to let her down.

But private thoughts were private, and not to be shared – certainly not with any 'Tom, Dick or

Harry' as Gran would say. Rita needed to talk to Gran, tell her what was going on, ask her what to do, whom to trust.

'Are you taking me to the hospital?' she asked.

'Yes, in a little while.' Wendy knew that the change of direction was deliberate. Rita did not want to talk. It was going to make her job very difficult. The child looked pale, and there were circles under her eyes. That was only to be expected, and gave no clue to what was going on under that slightly wary expression. Annie had said that Rita was withdrawn at dinner. She had hardly eaten a thing. Wendy suspected that Rita found the size of the family a bit overwhelming, after being with an elderly lady in a small flat. But that was just a guess; if the child wouldn't talk, how could she reassure her?

'Did you sleep all right, Rita? Do you like your room?'

Yes, Rita liked the room. 'It's all right.'

'How are you getting on with Jody?'

Rita shrugged. 'All right.' Jody had more or less ignored her. She had been polite, shown Rita where to put her things, asked her if she had anything to put on the walls. (Rita hadn't – Gran wouldn't allow posters at home, only proper framed pictures that she had approved.) Then she had asked what kind of music Rita liked. Rita, knowing that this was part of Jody's assessment of her, knew full well how important it was to choose what Jody would consider to be the right kind of music. Desperately she had said, 'I like most of what's in the charts.'

But Jody had not let her off the hook. Her eyes had narrowed slightly. 'But who do you really like?'

Rita had shrugged. Better to seem ignorant than choose the wrong thing. Jody had smiled slightly, and Rita could see she was being dismissed. The new girl was a dork; cheap clothes, old-fashioned hair style, no make-up, didn't even know what music she liked.

They had hardly exchanged any words at all after that. Rita felt small and shrivelled and frumpish next to this exotic creature who moved so gracefully, so surely, knowing where her place was and knowing too that she was secure in it.

'Just all right?' Wendy smiled, coaxing gently. 'Not "fine" or "great" or "awful". It doesn't give me much of a clue, does it?'

Rita shifted uncomfortably on the sofa. They were alone in the downstairs living room. Somewhere in the house people were talking, playing, washing-up, watching television. Everyone was in, but they were all staying tactfully clear of the living room while the new girl talked to her social worker. Presumably, from the intense 'I'm listening' expression on Wendy's face, Rita was supposed to pour her heart out. Unfortunately, this sort of awkwardness always brought out the worst in Rita. She was not used to sharing feelings, only covering them up. When pressed, the only way she knew out of such situations was to say something unexpected and divert attention.

'Well, Ah'll tell you,' she said, with a mock American drawl. 'I just lurv it here. Ah'm gonna treat them so nice, they ain't never gonna want me to leave. Yessir, this here is like Butlins and Disneyland all in one: the food of paradise. Wild

26

life, too – yessir, that there dawg is really a grizzly bear, in disguise.'

It was a satisfaction to see the desperate smile return. Wendy had no idea what to do with Rita when she was like this. Nor did Rita, but then she wasn't paid to sort out troublesome teenagers, was she?

'Making a joke of it only helps for a while, Rita. Sooner or later you have to face up to what's happening and deal with it.' Wendy was no longer smiling, just looking worried.

Rita squirmed inside; outwardly she simply shrugged her shoulders.

'Well, it's early days yet. I'm sure you'll find a place here for yourself, Rita.'

Rita silently doubted that. Dinner last night had been a nightmare. Everyone seemed to talk all the time in this house; there was never any peace and quiet. And at meal times the only impression Rita had was of hands: stretching across the table, grabbing food (in Charlie's case, grabbing from other people's plates!), squabbling over who had the most of something, trading in a way that would have shocked Gran ('You can have my salad, I'll have your bread'). It was total chaos, and she longed for the table at the flat, neatly laid for two, and the soft tunes of cutlery against plates and bowls. (They didn't talk much at the table, she and Gran.) But what was the point of telling Wendy all this? Was she supposed to ask the family to sit quietly at meal times because that's what Rita was used to? Of course not. It was something she had to put up with, like everything else that was different. Everything, in fact.

'In the normal run of things,' Wendy was saying, 'if you were coming into a family like this, we would have done it all very carefully. You would have met the family, come for the day, then a few weekends, then a week or so – you would have had plenty of time to get to know everyone and make a decision for yourself about whether this was the right place for you. I'm sorry that circumstances didn't permit that, Rita. It's an awful situation for you. What I'm trying to say is, if it doesn't work out, and you can't settle here, then you don't have to stay. You just need to keep me in touch with how things are going for you, so that I can help.'

Rita felt a bit sorry for Wendy. She was doing her best, and it wasn't fair to leave her floundering.

'I expect it'll be all right,' said Rita, lifting her head. It was the best she could offer. 'Can we go and see Gran now?'

Wendy hesitated. She wasn't sure if it was worth pursuing the interview any further. Rita was simply not ready to talk. But would she ever be?

The door was flung open, and Jason ran in, making engine noises. He was closely followed by Gnasher.

'Jason!' came Pete's voice, and Jason's hand flew to his mouth.

'Sorry – forgot,' he said, and turned to leave. 'Come on Gnasher.'

Gnasher, however, ignored the command. He padded over to Rita and rested his enormous head in her lap, looking up at her with large, soulful, red-rimmed eyes. She stroked his head.

'You've certainly made an impression there!' laughed Wendy.

It was true. Gnasher liked her, perhaps because she stroked him a lot and the others tended to pat him on the head and tell him to go away.

Pete popped his head round the door. 'Sorry about Jason,' he said. 'I think he was on a flying mission. He's an ace war-time hero today.'

'It's all right,' said Wendy. 'We've finished. I'm going to take Rita to see her grandmother now, and when I bring her back perhaps we can have a chat?'

About me, thought Rita. 'How is she getting on?' 'All right, as far as we can tell. Jody says she's . . . ' What would Jody say about her?

'Jolly good,' said Pete. 'Give your grandmother our best wishes, Rita, and we hope she's better soon.'

As he was a nurse, he would know there was little chance of that. Even Rita knew that a stroke as massive as Gran's was not shaken off like a cold or mended like a broken ankle. Gran's friend had had one, and it was weeks before she could go home. She had never been right since, Gran said. Pete worked at the hospital, he might even have gone to see Gran, suss out the situation for himself. If so, he was lying to her, the easy cheerful lies that adults told so often. They were forever telling you things were going to be all right when they knew they weren't. It was supposed to be comforting. It was the opposite, of course, because even when they told the truth you didn't know whether to believe them or not.

'I'll tell her,' said Rita. 'If she can understand me.'

Pete and Wendy exchanged looks. The child knew a bit more than she was letting on, then.

In the car, on the way to hospital, the familiar ache in Rita's shoulders and down her spine told her that she was tense. She tried to relax, breathe deeply, but it was not much help. She just wanted to get through as many days as it took until her life was her own again. She would have to switch onto automatic pilot and let it all wash over her. One day at a time, and finally the day would come when she would be back in the flat, with Gran snoring in an armchair in front of the television. Her own small, secure world would return. Her mind pushed aside the more probable outcome; she refused to accept that it could be any other way.

Gran had been moved from right beside the nurses' station to a bed in a small ward. That had to be a good sign. As they approached the bed, a nurse was just smoothing the sheets. She smiled at Rita and said, 'Your gran had quite a comfortable night. But I'm afraid she won't be able to say much. She can hear what you say, though, so don't worry about talking to her as much as you want.'

Rita nodded. The nurse moved briskly to the next bed. 'Morning, Mrs T. I'm just going to take your temperature, OK?'

Gran lay with her eyes closed. Her skin looked like old candle wax, scored with lines which criss-crossed her face. They had taken her teeth out, and her lips seemed to fall into her mouth like a scrunched-up rag. Her grey hair was smooth; some-one had combed it for her. She looked quite peaceful today. She also looked a small, fragile old lady.

Rita had never thought of Gran like that before. She had always been on the go, never ill, always busy. Often Rita would get home from school to find her engrossed in a fierce argument with her friends, who came round regularly to sit in the kitchen and drink tea while they sorted out the problems of the world. From the economic policies of the government to the doings of all the other families in their block, Gran always had something to say on the subject. There was not a single topic about which Gran didn't have strong views. She never missed the news on television, and would discuss what was happening with her granddaughter and ask Rita's opinion. Then she would give hers. Often Rita couldn't keep up, but she was amused at the fierceness of her gran's beliefs (and sometimes very irritated, too, although she didn't want to remember those times now).

It was hard to believe that this old lady, lying peaceful and submissive beneath a soft pink hospital cover, was really Gran. Rita knew that Wendy, who had never met her gran before the stroke, would not see the real person, only the painted shadow that lay before her now. But Rita knew who this person really was, and she would make sure that they didn't treat her like those other old ladies who sat nodding and smiling at her in the other beds. Gran was different. They would come to understand that, as Gran got better.

'Gran?' she whispered, taking Gran's thin hand into her own. 'It's Rita.'

Gran opened her eyes. Her mouth twisted on one side; perhaps it was a smile. A low growling sound came from her throat. Rita could only guess what she was trying to say, but she knew Gran well enough to know what sort of things would be on her mind.

'I'm staying with a really nice family,' she said. 'Wendy here, she's a social worker, and she found me a place to stay. They've got this enormous dog – a St Bernard it is, Gran. Huge thing, and very friendly. When you're better you'll see it, I expect.'

Gran looked bewildered. Rita wondered if she had gone too fast for her. She knew that a stroke made your brain sort of confused, so that things went down the wrong channels and got muddled up in your head.

'I'm fine,' she said. 'I don't want you to worry about me. Just get better.' That seemed to be the important thing to get through.

Gran's right arm lay limp and useless on the cover. She did not even grip Rita's hand. But the other hand moved across the cover and Rita took it. It squeezed her own gently. There was more growling. Gran seemed to know that she was not making sense. A look of irritation passed across her face. She moved her mouth to try again. Half her face was paralysed and she looked grotesque, like something from a horror film. Rita felt herself beginning to cry. 'Don't talk, Gran,' she said. 'There's no need.'

'Actually, Rita, the more she tries the better it is,' said Wendy. 'People who have strokes need to work very hard to get back their speech and movement, but it can be done with a lot of effort.' Mind you, she thought with a sinking heart, this was an elderly woman, already frail, and the stroke was a big one. It didn't look too good. She would have to have a word with Annie and Pete about how long they would be prepared to keep Rita, should the worse come to the worst.

'I'll bring a newspaper next time, Gran,' said Rita. 'I'll read you the news and you can tell me what you think. Like we do at home, eh?'

Gran looked bewildered again.

'Rita, would you like to go and watch the television in the day room for a bit? I'd like to have a word with your gran myself.'

About me, thought Rita. But what right has she to discuss my life behind my back?

'I don't like television much,' she said.

'How about a drink, then? We passed the cafeteria on the way in, I'm sure you could find it easily. I'll have a quick word with your gran, and then when you come back I'll go and get a coffee myself, and you can spend some time on your own with her before we go.'

'Not thirsty,' said Rita. 'Anyway, I want to stay with Gran.'

There was nothing to stop Wendy coming back without Rita if she wanted to say something that badly, but since Gran wouldn't understand and couldn't say anything back, Rita couldn't see the need. She wasn't leaving Gran with this woman who hardly knew her and would make all sorts of assumptions about her if Rita wasn't there to set her straight.

Wendy could see she was getting nowhere. Rita was an intelligent girl. She said very little but Wendy could almost see her brain whirring and clicking, putting things into place and sizing up people and situations. Perhaps she should come clean.

She leaned over towards the old lady. 'Mrs Dennison, I just want you to know that Rita is in a good home. Annie and Pete Brown are very experienced foster parents, and there are other children to keep Rita company, too. Now, we need to go to the flat, Mrs Dennison. We took just enough clothes for Rita for a few days, and she'll need some more things. Also, we're going to have to look through any address books or things like that if we find them, because we want to tell your daughter, Kathleen, about you being ill. I'm sorry we have to do this, Mrs Dennison, but I hope you can understand that it is necessary.'

Gran didn't seem to take it in. Rita looked at Wendy angrily. 'You can't go through her private things,' she said. 'That's surely not allowed.'

'Rita, I know this is hard. I gather your gran and your mother are in touch from time to time. I think your mother has a right to know what's happening, don't you?'

'You're wrong. Gran never hears from Kathleen – she doesn't even know where she is!' said Rita.

Wendy swallowed. This was going to be more difficult than she had feared. It hadn't occurred to her that the child would have no inkling of the contact that had been going on between Kathleen and her grandmother. Mrs Dennison's friends had told her that Kathleen had dumped the small baby on Mrs Dennison and disappeared. But they had also told her that very occasionally, perhaps twice a year, Mrs Dennison received a telephone call from Kathleen – checking that she was still alive, was the way they put it. Kathleen had clearly made no effort to contact Rita, and that seemed to suggest that there was little hope of her taking custody of Rita if Mrs Dennison died.

'I think your gran might know where Kathleen is, Rita,' she said carefully. 'I think she might have a clue written down somewhere that would help us to find Kathleen. It's worth a try, anyway.'

She meant it. She was going to find Kathleen, and if there were no clues in the flat Rita didn't doubt that Wendy knew other things to try too. They were going to dredge up the ghost of a mother Rita had thought and dreamed and wondered about all her life, and give her flesh. Rita lay her head on Gran's chest and wept silently into her hair.

4

Rita's sleep was filled, not so much with dreams, but with images of people. Jody smiled that awful, slow smile, like a wolf sizing up its dinner; Wendy offered her mysterious-looking packages she was afraid to take in her hand. Pete and Annie joined hands and walked away from her; Mark took both her hands and danced Rita round the room, which kept changing from her own flat to a bare white room and back again. She was confused, troubled. Finally, she realized that the white room was in a hospital, and there was a bed in the room with a figure lying on it, covered with a sheet. Rita approached. 'It's your mother, Kathleen,' said Jody with a smile. 'Say hello.' Rita twitched the sheet – Gran's eyes stared at her, wide open and lifeless.

Rita woke with a shock, starting from sleep as though someone had fired a shot. For a moment she didn't know where she was. Jody's bed, rumpled and empty, reminded her. She was with the Browns, and an outing was planned. Jason had told her about it the night before, his face aglow with excitement. They were taking a picnic. A whole day of happy families. Rita wondered if she could develop a convincing headache, and whether they would let her stay at home if she did. Probably someone would stay at home with her. It might even be Jody, press-ganged to keep her company because they were the same age, and therefore it was assumed they would 'get on'. In fact Jody had still hardly said a word to Rita, and Rita had certainly not volunteered any conversation.

Downstairs she could hear the clattering of breakfast things in the dining room. Yesterday they had all eaten breakfast at different times, fending for themselves. Today it sounded as though everyone was getting ready to eat together. At least if Rita was out all day no-one could spring surprises on her – like Kathleen showing up on the doorstep to claim her long-lost daughter, for instance. She tumbled out of bed, showered as quickly as she could and went down.

Everyone was there. Annie looked up and smiled at her as she came in. 'Morning, Rita.'

'Morning, sleepyhead,' said Mark. 'Jason was all set to storm in and wash your face with a cold flannel. I stopped him. I hope you're grateful.'

'Yes, I am,' said Rita. She smiled at Jason.

'Weeta,' said Charlie. For a moment, Rita thought he was referring to his bowl of weetabix, at least a quarter of which was around his mouth while the rest seemed to be on his bib, dropping in small globules back into the bowl. She could hardly bear to look at him. He said 'Weeta!' again, with more urgency, and she realized that Charlie was calling her by name.

'He's saying my name!' she said, pleased.

'Weeta!' chuckled Charlie.

Annie nodded at him and clapped her hands.

'That's right, Charlie. Rita. He's glad to see you. Poor little chap must wonder who's going to be there when he wakes up in the morning. Sometimes I have to count you myself, to keep track of who's here and who's not. Ah well.'

Rita looked across at Jody. Jody gave her a brief, uninterested smile and returned her attention to the grapefruit she was dissecting.

'We've decided to go to Forester Park, up in the hills,' said Pete. 'Picnic lunch. Are you up to a day out?'

It was his way of checking whether she was OK after seeing her gran looking so poorly the night before. Rita nodded. 'All right,' she said.

'Don't bowl us over with your enthusiasm,' said Jody.

'Now now, my little wasp, pull your sting back in,' smiled Pete.

Jody pulled a face at him.

'I'm sorry,' said Rita miserably. 'I didn't mean to sound as if – '

'Nor did Jody,' interrupted Mark. 'She just operates her mouth without engaging her brain sometimes. When are we going, Dad?'

Pete looked at his watch. 'What do you think, Annie? Shall we leave about an hour for clearing up and getting the little ones ready? The food's all sorted – Mum and Dad are bringing it with them, we've just got to put in some fruit and things to drink.'

'Yes, an hour should be fine,' said Annie. 'Jason and Rita, will you wash up, please? Jody, you'd better go to the shop and buy a couple of bottles of Coke or something. I've got plenty of apple juice, so that should about do it. Mark, can you run the hoover round downstairs? That blasted dog's hair gets everywhere. Pete, you take Charlie and I'll take Adam. OK?'

The family moved into operation like a well-oiled machine and Rita felt a glimmer of belonging as she was naturally slotted in to play her part in it.

Rosie and her husband came while Rita was washing up. Jason threw down his tea towel and raised his arms for a hug with a beaming smile. Rosie hugged Rita, too, taking her by surprise. 'This is Annie's dad, George,' she said. 'George, this is Rita.'

'How do,' said George. He was quite small for a man, only about Rosie's height, and he looked sort of round and jolly. He had very little hair on his head and seemed to be compensating for that with a white moustache and a bushy beard. I bet he gets asked to play Father Christmas at nursery schools, thought Rita.

'Are you surviving, then?' asked George. 'They're all nutters here, you know. If you're not mad now, you will be by the time you leave.'

Rita laughed. 'I'm getting used to it a bit,' she said, and was surprised to discover that this was actually true.

George and Rosie joined in with the washing-up and Rosie scrubbed the table and work surfaces and cleaned the sink too, while Jason and Rita were sent upstairs to tidy the babies' room ('I don't need to go up there to know it'll be a hell-hole,' said Rosie) and then to help George peg out the washing.

'Mum, you are a marvel,' said Annie when she came down to find everything done. Adam lay contentedly in her arms. 'What would I do without you?'

'Sink,' said Rosie briefly, and gave her daughter a kiss.

'Let me see that baby,' said George. He took Adam and held him up in the air. 'Look at the length on him,' he said. 'I'll swear he's grown just in this last week. He'll be a big chap.'

Rita envied Annie the closeness she had with her parents. It was a strange family. Rosie and George seemed to be as fond of the foster children as if they were their own grandchildren. Rita wondered if it would have been different if Annie and Pete had their own child, perhaps a daughter, someone like Rita. If Rita had been born into this family, she would have had two proper parents, and this couple would have been her gran and grandad. Her life would have been so different. But her place had been chosen by some mysterious hand of fate. She felt the unfairness of it, and felt too the guilt of knowing that her wishful thinking was disloyal to Gran, who had given her everything she could.

Rita decided that she would have to do her best to enjoy this day out with the Browns. On Monday Wendy would begin to ferret around for information about Kathleen, and who knew what would happen then? The reappearance of Kathleen into her life hovered over Rita like a swinging axe from a horror movie.

Finally everything was ready, and the family assembled in the hall to sort out who was going in whose car. Gnasher, who was also to be included, had been shut out of the house while everything was loaded in. He knew something was afoot, and was barking furiously outside the back door. There was an enormous amount of luggage as well: a double buggy for Charlie and Adam; a big bag of nappies, creams, lotions and so on; two tennis rackets and a tube of tennis balls; two picnic hampers; a large coolbox containing the drinks, and a carrier bag full of fruit; Gnasher's huge steel water bowl, and a plastic container full of water.

'Where's the kitchen sink?' chuckled George. 'We're surely not going without that!'

It seemed impossible that they fitted into two cars, but they did. George took Rosie, Jody, Jason and Mark and Rita found herself sandwiched in between two baby seats in Pete's car, with Charlie and Adam. All the luggage which did not fit in George's boot was piled on to the floor beneath the baby seats. This seemed odd to Rita, since the car was an enormous estate, then she remembered Gnasher. He presumably needed the luggage space all to himself.

'Stand back everybody – I'm letting Gnasher out!' called Pete. There was a good humoured wail of 'Oh no, the Beast!' from the back of George's car. Pete opened the hatchback door of the estate and went into the house, leaving the front door wide open. Rita turned in her seat to watch. There was a moment's silence – Gnasher had stopped barking. Then, like a hairy tornado, Gnasher charged out of the house and jumped into the car, crashing into the back seat and flopping down with all his eleven stone to claim his rightful place on the family outing. The car rocked. Rita had never seen the lumbering old dog move so fast.

They set off, and apart from Gnasher's insistence

on standing up now and then and looking over the back seat, which meant he dribbled down the back of Rita's neck and necessitated complicated measures to keep the babies out of the firing line of his saliva, the journey was not too bad. They parked in a quiet part of the park and set up camp. Annie and Rosie threw two blankets on to the grass and settled down to chat. Adam was in his buggy, watching the trees move in the breeze. Pete and Mark wandered off with Jason to collect pine cones, Gnasher in tow, and George offered to supervise Charlie at the sandpit nearby. Jody challenged Rita to a game of tennis.

'There's a tennis court over there, through those trees,' she pointed. 'Don't worry if you're not any good; if you can hit the ball at all, we'll be able to get some sort of game going.'

Rita suppressed a smile when she heard the superior tone in Jody's voice. 'OK,' she said. 'I'll do my best.' The beautiful little madam had a shock coming to her, with any luck.

Rita was in the school tennis team; last year she had been captain. It was generally agreed that she had real talent. Where it came from, nobody knew. Her father, probably, since Gran's amazement at her talent seemed to suggest she had not inherited it from Kathleen.

Without a word, Rita listened to Jody explaining the way the toss of the racket worked. Rita won, and chose service. She listened meekly while Jody reminded her that she had two goes at a serve, and showed her where to serve from and to. She walked to the point Jody had indicated and watched Jody walk to the other side of the net and take up the ready position.

Rita bounced the ball a couple of times, judging its age and springiness. 'They always do this at Wimbledon,' she called over to Jody with the sheepish smile of someone who had no idea what she was doing.

Then she threw the tennis ball into the air and served. Jody didn't even move; the ball was so fast and hard that she barely knew it had come past her.

'Wow!' she called. 'Well done. Fifteen love.'

I bet you think it was a fluke, thought Rita. You're about to find out your mistake. She served again, stretching up into the sunlight and whamming the ball with her racket.

By the end of the match Jody could be in no doubt that Rita knew how to play tennis. She had lost every point except three. It was a humiliating defeat. Rita even began to feel sorry for her, towards the end. But as Jody came round the net afterwards, Rita was surprised to see her mouth stretch into a tense smile.

'You horrible little thing!' she laughed. 'You let me witter on about how to play tennis and then you slaughter me. I'm so embarrassed I just don't know where to put myself!'

'Sorry,' said Rita. She hadn't wanted to make Jody dislike her even more, she just didn't want to feel like the poor little lost girl all the time.

'Oh, I deserved it,' laughed Jody. 'Serves me right for being so snooty. You can really play, Rita. Wow. You'd better play Dad after lunch – he's the only one who'll stand a chance against you.'

Rita was perplexed by the sudden generosity and affection that Jody possessed alongside the sharp temper and the biting observations she enjoyed making about people. She couldn't figure out exactly where she stood with this gorgeous, confident creature who could snipe at her one minute and take her arm the next. But she felt a glow of pleasure at having proved she could do something well.

The picnic lunch was chaos: hands everywhere; trading of food; drinks passing round, spilling; bags of crisps sailing through the air, and the ever-present Gnasher trying to make a charge on to the blankets whenever he thought no-one was looking, and retiring mournfully to a respectful distance whenever he was shooed away. But Rita no longer found this large family so overwhelming. She even managed to join in, although she drew the line at Charlie's half-chewed banana which he cheerfully tried to feed her.

'Nice, Weeta. Nice 'nana.'

'Mmm, lovely,' said Rita, pretending to eat the soggy mess squelched into the chubby little fist. 'Now Charlie have some.'

Charlie grinned and stuffed his mouth.

'You've got a real way with him, hasn't she, Annie?' said Rosie. Annie murmured agreement. 'You'd never know you didn't have little brothers and sisters, yourself, Rita,' said Rosie approvingly.

In the afternoon, Jody having told everyone about Rita's amazing skill with a tennis racket, the whole family gathered at the court to watch Pete and Rita play a game. Rita had not wanted to do this, but gave in to the determination to see her play. Pete was quite good, and much stronger than Rita. His serves were very difficult to return. Nonetheless, although she didn't win the match, Rita did manage to win one set and was quite satisfied with her performance. She knew Pete hadn't made any allowances for her by the way he looked at her when the match was over. 'My word, Rita,' he said. 'You're going to win Wimbledon one day.'

'No,' said Rita calmly. 'I'm not going to be that good. But I might make the British team.'

Pete smiled and patted her on the back. 'Well done,' he said. 'That's the first confident statement I've heard you make.'

Rita didn't understand what he meant, but she knew it was nothing nasty. She accepted the admiration and congratulations of everyone else with real happiness. It was the first time she had felt happy since Gran's stroke, but it was all too brief. The memory of her Gran's gaping mouth and confused stare snaked back to haunt her.

'The others are going to follow the nature trail,' said Annie. 'Do you want to go with them, or stay behind with me and the babies?'

'I'll stay and help with them if you like,' said Rita shyly.

'Great. Actually I think Charlie is going to have a snooze, but I'd be glad of the company.'

Charlie did indeed fall asleep, with his head on Mark's jacket and a travel rug over him. Adam fed peacefully on his bottle in Annie's arms.

'It's so quiet!' smiled Rita.

'Yes. I suppose we must seem a riotous lot to you, Rita. You must be used to a lot more peace and quiet than we can offer, I'm afraid.'

45

'It's all right,' said Rita. 'I'm getting to quite like it.'

'Yes, you do look a lot more cheerful today. That's good.'

Rita took a deep breath. 'Jason likes living with you, doesn't he?'

'Yes, he does. We like him, too. He had a very bad time at home, and no-one really stood up for him, and yet he manages to smile and enjoy life. He's got real courage, that little chap.'

'He's not staying with you, though, is he?'

'No. He's going to be adopted. Actually the social worker called yesterday; he thinks he's found some-one. A family in Somerset.'

Rita, who had been brought up not to pry and not to ask questions, did not know how to ask why Jason was moving on.

Annie saved her the trouble. 'What's up, Rita? Is something bothering you?'

'I was just wondering why – '

'Why he can't stay here?'

Rita nodded.

'Rita, there's nothing Pete and I would like more than to keep Jason – and a dozen more like him, if we had the room. But it's not as simple as that.'

She sat Adam upright and rubbed his back until he burped, and then settled him into her arm for the rest of his feed. 'You see, Jason needs a family where he can be the youngest, or even the only child. He's happy here at the moment because, frankly, compared to what the poor little boy had before *anything* would seem like heaven. But as time goes on and his past starts to catch up with him, he'll need a lot of time and love. This family in

Somerset have two grown-up sons and no other children. The whole family are keen to have Jason – think how much love and attention he'll get from them. We could stop fostering, of course, which would put Jason into the same position here. But Pete and I feel that it's important to have people like us available to children for a little while, to help them over bad patches. If we stopped short-term fostering there'd be children who needed a safe harbour for a while who would be out in the cold.'

'Like me,' said Rita. 'I needed a safe harbour.'

'Exactly. And there were no other foster families at all available when you came into care. So you can see what the situation is.'

'Yes, I see. But poor Jason.'

'He'll be fine. They won't just come and take him away, Rita. They'll come to visit the whole family, first of all. Then they'll maybe take Jason to the park, out to tea, that sort of thing. If all that goes well, Jason will go to their house for a weekend, then perhaps a few days, go on holiday with them. If all that goes well, the visits will become more frequent, and his stays with them a bit longer. Meanwhile, back at our home we'll be gently preparing him for moving on. When the time comes for the adoption to go through, Jason will be more than happy with his new parents, I promise you.'

'I didn't realize it worked like that,' said Rita. She had felt like a flower torn up by the roots when *she* arrived at the Browns' house; she had assumed it was like that for everyone.

'What about you, Rita?' asked Annie suddenly.

'Me?'

Annie wobbled the bottle across Adam's lips. He

had fallen asleep. She put him over her shoulder and rubbed his back gently. 'You're a very intelligent young woman. I'm sure you have thought your situation through. You know that your grandmother may not be able to look after you if or when she comes out of hospital. If that should happen, I want you to know that you have a place here as long as you need it.'

Rita squirmed uncomfortably. The truth was, it had occurred to her that if the Browns only took people for a little while, she would have to go through all this again if Gran didn't get better soon. She hadn't wanted to ask how long she could stay. But once again Annie had seemed to know what was on her mind. It must have happened to lots of kids before Rita. She studied her trainers, smoothing the laces with her fingers. 'Thank you,' she said politely. 'I hope it won't come to that.'

'So do I. For your sake, not ours.'

Rita thought of her gran, lying in the hospital, and wondered what she would say if she could hear this conversation. She sent a message on the mental airwaves, reassuring her gran that she had not given up on her, that she had not forgotten her place, which was with Gran. Just get better, Gran. And please, get better before they decide to try and find Kathleen.

5

The day out cheered Rita. She had not felt like an outsider at all. Mark had played tennis with her – he was pretty useless, as he himself admitted, and she beat him easily. Jody had been much warmer towards her than she had been at the Browns' house, and Jason had insisted on holding her hand at almost every opportunity. Rita felt a bit guilty about having enjoyed herself with Gran so sick in the hospital, but at least she had managed to push her fears about Kathleen to the back of her mind.

In the car on the way back, Pete told her that they would be passing near the hospital.

'I think it's important for you to go and see your gran every day, Rita,' he said. 'So we thought we could drop you off at the hospital, pay a visit to some friends who live in the nurses' home and pick you up afterwards. What do you think?'

'That would be great,' said Rita happily. She fished a comb out of her back pocket and started to tug at her hair.

'Here,' said Annie, handing her a hairbrush over her shoulder. 'I think this might be easier with hair that length.'

'Thanks.' Rita had left her brush at the flat, and

had been too shy to ask if she could borrow one, or have some money. Her hair was tangled, and it was quite a job, but by the time they reached the hospital car park it was smooth. It felt so good to have properly brushed hair; strange, she thought, how little things can make you feel so much better.

'I'll come up to the ward to collect you,' said Pete as they got out of the car. 'It won't be longer than an hour – Adam and Charlie will need feeding. OK?'

'Yes. Thanks.'

Rita turned to go into the hospital. Pete called her back. She looked with horror at the five pound note he was offering her.

'Pocket money, Rita. Thought you might appreciate it, to buy your gran something at the hospital shop.'

'I can't take that!' said Rita, aghast. 'Gran wouldn't like it.'

'Rita, it's pocket money. Doesn't your gran give you pocket money?'

Yes, she did: two pounds every Saturday. It was all she could afford. But money from Gran and money from a man she hardly knew were totally different things.

'I don't want it – thanks anyway. Gran won't be expecting anything.' She felt so embarrassed she wanted to shrivel up. Pete was holding out the money.

'I think you've got the wrong end of the stick,' said Annie gently. 'We get an allowance from the social services to look after you, Rita. Part of that money is for pocket money. If we don't give it to you, well, it will be like we're stealing it from you. You see?'

No, she didn't see. Gran had very strong views on taking handouts and charity. She hadn't let Rita have school dinners, even though Rita could have had them for free. She had called them 'charity'. Rita, who had only seen that the dinners were nicer than her packed lunch and that most of her friends got their dinners for free, had tried to argue. But Gran had left her in no doubt that people had to make their own way in the world. Rita accepted that she couldn't pay her way while she was living with the Browns. But she didn't think Gran would like the idea of taking money from them.

'Please, take it Rita. We want you to have it. You've earned it, helping with the little ones today. If you won't take it as pocket money, take it as wages, eh?'

Rita took the money and tucked it into her jeans. 'Thanks,' she muttered, but she didn't believe the bit about wages. She only took the money because she didn't want a scene. ''Bye.' She ran across the car park and into the hospital.

'That is a weird child,' said Annie, shaking her head.

'Old-fashioned, that's all,' said Pete. He looked thoughtful. 'She needs a bit more contact with younger people, maybe. Needs to think for herself a bit more, become her own person. That old gran of hers seems to rule with a rod of iron, doesn't she?'

'Mmm. Rita loves her, though. And she doesn't seem to realize that she herself is . . . well, a bit odd compared to other children of her age.'

'I wonder Jody hasn't pointed it out by now,' said Pete grimly.

'She probably has,' smiled Annie. 'But that might not be such a bad thing. I know Jody speaks before she thinks, but her heart's in the right place. Maybe she'll take Rita in hand, inject a bit of life into her.'

'I don't think things are going too well between them so far,' said Pete. 'Still, it's early days. I don't think Rita's gran is going to be coming out very soon – if at all.'

The object of Pete's concern was at that moment passing by the hospital shop. She stopped to look in the window. There were beautiful arrangements of dried flowers, and 'Get Well' cards with feathers on them, and many other pretty things. Perhaps it wouldn't be such a bad idea to get Gran a little present. It would cheer her up.

'Hello,' said the woman running the shop. She was quite elderly. She had a red overall on, and a white badge which said, 'Friends of the Darwin Memorial Hospital'. 'Can I help you?'

'I want to choose something for my gran – she's on Evelyn Ward.'

'Ah, that's nice. Well, we have fresh flowers, dried flowers – they're a bit expensive, mind – and chocolates, stationery and so on. You have a look around. Don't take too long though, dear; I'm just about to close.' She smiled at Rita and turned away to take the big vases of fresh flowers out of the window.

Right in front of Rita was a display of soap and talcum powder. There were also a few bottles of very exotic-looking bubble bath. Rita picked one up to look at the price sticker. Gran loved to have a bubble bath as a special treat. Nine pounds fifty! She moved on to look at some less expensive ones, but by comparison to the first bottle they looked cheap and tacky.

It wasn't fair. Gran had scrimped and scraped by all her life, and now she was worn out and ill and had never had the chance of a few little luxuries.

A small whisper somewhere in her head told her to slip it into her jacket. The old lady was busy, she'd never know. But Rita fought it. How could she give her gran a stolen present? A gift was supposed to be something you had bought with your own money. Ah, but the five pounds isn't your own money is it, Rita? said the little voice. It's Pete who's buying the present, not you. At least if you took it, it would really come from you.

Nervously, Rita looked over her shoulder. The old lady caught her eye. 'Chosen yet?'

Rita smiled shyly, 'Not yet – it's difficult to decide.'

The old lady's heart warmed to the girl – such a nice-looking little thing, not like these hard brassy girls who came in these days, with their permed hair and earrings swinging. 'Well, look – I'll give you five more minutes while I cash up the till. But that's it.'

'Thank you,' said Rita. 'That's very kind of you.'

What a well-mannered child, thought the lady, and settled to her task.

Rita slipped the bottle of expensive bubbles into her jacket, and picked up the cheaper one. 'I'll have these,' she said, and the lady smiled. 'Good choice,' she beamed. 'There's nothing nicer, when you're away from home and feeling poorly, than a bit of luxury. I hope your grandmother's better soon, dear.'

'Thank you.' The woman's kindness made Rita feel bad even before she left the shop. By the time she had reached the staircase her conscience was screaming 'Stop! Thief!' so loud she was surprised it couldn't actually be heard. Why on earth had she done that? Rita was absolutely disgusted with herself, especially at the thought that she had planned to give this stolen thing to Gran, who had never done a dishonest thing in all her life.

She couldn't give it to Gran, of course she couldn't. She would have to dispose of it. The bin would be the easiest, and yet Rita couldn't bring herself to do it. Whether this was fear of being seen or a desire to keep the stuff for herself, it was difficult to say. But when she reached Evelyn Ward, Rita still had the cheap bottle clasped in her hand and the expensive bottle burning against her ribs inside the jacket.

When she told the nurse on duty whom she had come to visit, she was told that she would be really encouraged to see how well her gran was doing. 'Sat up for a little while, she did, and she's doing amazingly well with conversation,' said the nurse. 'Go on round – third bed on the right.'

Gran still looked waxy, but she was awake, and she recognized Rita. Her mouth twisted into something resembling a smile. Rita saw with dismay that her face still didn't move properly. Pete had told her that the first two days were very important in stroke recovery, because that's when the biggest improvements usually occurred, if there were going to be any. Gran's right arm still lay on the cover, absolutely still.

'Hello, Gran. You're looking better,' said Rita, and kissed her on the cheek.

'Rita,' said Gran.

'Yes, Gran. Rita.' Her heart lifted; at least Gran could talk.

'Daughter?' said Gran. She looked confused.

'Granddaughter, Gran. I'm your granddaughter. Rita. We live in the flat, thirty-two Arundel House, remember? It's just you and me, Gran.'

Gran shook her head impatiently. Was this because she knew all that already, or because Rita had misunderstood her? She couldn't tell.

'Daughter?' said Gran again. She looked around.

She was asking for Kathleen. Rita felt the room shift around her. Please, no. She couldn't cope with that.

'Look what I've brought you, Gran,' she said, and put the bottle of bubble bath into Gran's left hand, the one that still worked. As she leaned over to do this, the stolen one pressed into her, under her jacket. Gran looked at the bottle and puzzled over it, trying to work out what it was.

'Bubble bath, Gran. You put it in the bath, and it smells lovely and makes bubbles which clean you while you just lay back. Remember?'

Gran nodded. 'Sugar,' she said, and then added hurriedly, 'No. Soap. Soap.'

Rita's heart sank. She could speak all right, but she sounded very strange. And what she was saying was even stranger.

'How are you, Gran? Are they treating you all

right? Do you want me to get you anything?' asked Rita as cheerily as she could.

Gran waved her left hand frantically, the index finger pressed onto the thumb. Rita took the hand in hers and tried to soothe her, but she became even more agitated. 'Pulpy stuff,' she said, 'for write.'

'Stop it, Gran. Please, stop!' This madness frightened her. She needed Gran too much to stand watching her slip away from the world like this.

The nurse she had seen the day before noticed her distress and came over. 'All right?'

'She's just talking nonsense,' said Rita, trying not to cry. 'Is she going mad?'

The nurse shook her head. 'No, she's doing very well. And she can understand every word you say, isn't that right, Mrs Dennison?'

Gran waved her left hand up and down, and Rita saw that she was nodding as well.

'Why won't she talk to me, then?' asked Rita.

'It's not that simple. She can try and try, but sometimes the words just won't come. Or she knows what she wants to say, but can't think of the right word. Her brain sorts out another word, perhaps a similar one or one that has a link with what she wants. It's a bit of a puzzle working it out sometimes.'

'Oh.'

The nurse patted her shoulder. 'Do you want me to stay, and try to interpret?'

'No thanks. I'll just sit.'

'All right. Now don't you worry. Your gran's a fighter, and she's on her way back to us.' The nurse moved on to another patient.

Gran didn't look like much of a fighter at the

moment. The effort of trying to speak had tired her, and she closed her eyes. Rita sat, stroking her hand.

'Please get better, Gran,' she said. 'I really need you. I need to tell you things . . . not things you should worry about, Gran,' she added, horrified by the thought that she might make Gran worse, 'but, you know, I miss talking to you. The Browns are great, and they're making me feel at home. But they're not you, Gran. I need to talk to someone who knows me – and I need you to tell me what to do. So get better soon, will you? Please.'

She sat for a long time watching her grandmother sleep, and trying to imagine what life would be like without her. It was impossible. All around her nurses bustled, patients coughed and moaned, cheery greetings from other visitors crossed the ward. But Gran didn't move for a long time. Then her eyes opened wide, suddenly. She was trying to say something. Rita leaned forward eagerly. 'Yes, Gran? What is it? Try, Gran. Try really hard to tell me. . . .'

'Daughter,' breathed Gran. 'Kay, Kayleen. Kayleen.'

Tears stung Rita's eyes, but didn't fall. Her grief at seeing her gran like this gave way to a cold rush of anger. When she needed her grandmother most, when she had worried herself half to death, Gran was thinking of Kathleen. She had told Rita they were better off without her, and expected Rita to ask no questions at all. And all the time she and Kathleen had been in touch with each other, perhaps talking about her. And when Gran needed someone badly, it was Kathleen she thought of. Not content with abandoning her as a baby and leaving

57

her with no chance of a proper family, this Kathleen woman had stolen Rita's place in her Gran's thoughts.

'I think she's asleep, Rita.' Pete was crouching beside her. 'And so are you, only with your eyes open. You were miles away. Are you OK?'

Rita nodded. 'She spoke.'

'Yes, I know. I had a word with the Sister on the way in. They think she'll recover very well, in time. She'll have a bit of trouble with her arm and leg, but they'll teach her ways of coping. Most important thing is, they think she'll be able to go back home in the end, with a home help. That means you and she will be back together. That's great, isn't it?'

It was all Rita had been waiting to hear until ten minutes ago. Now, it didn't even pierce the armour she had put on. She shrugged. 'I suppose so.' She got up and walked out of the ward, Pete following in confusion. She hadn't even said goodbye. She remembered that halfway down the stairs, but why go back? She would only disappoint, again. She was not Kathleen.

Pete followed her down the stairs and along the corridor. As they passed the hospital shop Rita felt the bottle burning, and she zipped her jacket even tighter.

'Rita, what did your gran say? Did you have trouble understanding her?'

Rita nodded.

'That'll get better. You'll see, tomorrow.'

Rita nodded again. 'I know.' Tomorrow, or the next day, she wouldn't be able to pretend she didn't know what Gran meant. Even if she could, others

58

would understand. Pulpy stuff for writing – pen and paper. She was going to write it down. Then the hunt for Kathleen would be on.

Pete and Annie's best efforts to get Rita to say something failed on the way home. Even Charlie couldn't get a reaction, and gave up, returning to the tiny box of raisins he had been given at the nurses' home.

There was an almost festive atmosphere at the Browns, with everyone chipping in to make dinner. Rosie and George were staying, and it had been decided to have a real feast to finish off the day. Rita couldn't face it. 'Sorry,' she said, as soon as they got in. 'I'm really tired, and not very hungry. Do you mind if I go to bed?' She went upstairs, and quickly took the bottle from her jacket and dumped it in the drawer which was built in to her bed. Knowing that someone would be sure to come after her, in this family where no-one was allowed to suffer alone, she got into her pyjamas as quickly as she could and lay down.

There was a gentle tap on the door, and Annie came in. 'Do you want to talk?' she said, sitting on the end of the bed.

Rita shook her head. 'Just tired.'

'Well, we're here if you change your mind. Goodnight, Rita.'

She hadn't tried to persuade and she hadn't persisted. Rita had rather hoped she would. Although she didn't want to talk about Kathleen and her gran, Rita knew that if someone really pushed her she would cave in. Gran would have gone on and on until she was worn down, and confessed. Annie was leaving her a choice. But what choice? The

59

choice to wander in no-man's land, denied her rightful place and unable to fit in any other. She was adrift, and alone.

6

Rita saw her gran twice more over the weekend that followed, but nothing more was said about Kathleen. She was relieved about this, but felt all the time as though something was hanging over her. All weekend she hung around the house, pretending to read or watch TV. Jody invited her to go into town with her and her friends, but it was a reluctant offer and Rita could tell Jody was glad when Rita said no.

Rita spent the whole two days and two nights waiting for the telephone, or the doorbell that would herald the announcement that Kathleen had been found. What then? Would she insist on coming to see Rita, or would she say she had washed her hands of her years ago and had no interest in her now? Both options were unbearable to Rita.

On Monday morning, at seven o'clock, Rita was awoken by a very loud alarm – Jody's. She didn't want to wake up, but the bell was persistent. Rita raised her head. Her hair, as usual, was a tangled mess. She had not bothered to plait it before going to sleep, and it was in knots. Pushing it back, Rita sat up and swung her legs on to the floor. The threadbare patch on the right knee of her pyjamas would finally give up the ghost any day now. Rita doubted Gran would be able to afford new ones. What happened about her pension when she was in hospital? Would she still get it? Rita didn't know, and couldn't ask anyone. It would look money-grabbing. Gran said it was very rude to talk about money at all, still less your own lack of it.

On the other side of the room, Jody rose from her bed like a young gazelle. Her thick, carefully-cut hair swung into place as though it had just been combed. Even first thing in the morning she looked immaculate. It wasn't fair.

'You look like something rising from the bottom of the ocean,' she said casually, not realizing – or caring – that Rita would be hurt by the remark. 'I bags the shower – if Mark hasn't beaten me to it.' She gathered up a little cluster of pots and a hairbrush.

Rita fingered the almost bare patch on her pyjamas. Jody would have thrown them away long ago, if they were hers. You could tell from the sidelong glance she gave them as she passed Rita on the way to the door, in her flowing nightdress with satin and lace trim. They were pyjamas for a child, really, not a teenager. Actually, Rita was quite fond of them, in the way that she loved many of her clothes. They were a part of her, and they were comfy. They also came from home. But being with Jody made her look at everything with different eyes, almost as though she were someone else. She was plain, and lumpy and awkward. She didn't know what to wear, or say, or do. Simply, she did not fit anywhere except in her own place with her own gran. There, she was Rita, who was a laugh to be with, a good friend and talented at tennis. Here, she was a poor lone little thing. It was like climbing out of your own skin and trying on a different one. Rita didn't like it at all.

There was a knock on the door. 'OK Rita?' smiled Annie. 'Back to school today. I think we'll need to leave at quarter past eight to get there in time. Breakfast's on the table – help yourself to what you want.' Then she was gone. 'Jason, get a move on. Mark, turn that stereo *down!*'

The whole house was in pandemonium. Adam was wailing for his bottle, Charlie was making patterns with his cereal and spreading sticky handfuls of it everywhere. Pete was hammering on the door of the shower upstairs ('No, Jody, I will *not* go downstairs. You've been in there long enough. What? I don't *want* a bath instead. You've got two minutes, and that's it!')

Annie looked bad-tempered when she came downstairs, closely followed by Jason with a very woeful look on his face.

'I told you to put everything from school in the laundry basket at the end of last half-term,' Annie was saying. 'And in any case, you should have got all your stuff ready last night. If I'd known about your blasted PE things then, I could have *done* something about it.'

'I forgot,' said Jason mournfully. 'Mrs Morris won't let me do PE if my stuff's dirty, and it's apparatus today.' He started to cry. Rita moved towards him, but Annie snapped, 'Go and get the washing powder from the laundry room. I'll wash it out and try to iron it dry. You'll just have to wear it damp, that's all. And stop whinging, Jason. Next time, get your act together. And get your stuff ready for school the night before, and not at the last minute like this.'

Rita felt a bit scared of this new Annie, with the snappy voice and fierce eyes. Charlie, too, looked upset. His bottom lip turned down, and trembled. 'It's all right, Charlie,' soothed Rita. She wiped his face with the damp flannel kept in readiness at the back of his highchair. It was soon crusted with a mush of cereal and milk.

'Thanks,' said Annie. 'Look, can you keep an eye on him while I wash Jason's stuff – and put some bread in the toaster for Jason. He can get his own cereal.' She disappeared, snatching the powder from Jason's hand as he arrived in the doorway with it.

Rita slotted the bread into the toaster and pushed it down. Jason was sitting at the table like a little mouse, not moving. Two huge tears spilled out onto his cheek. 'Don't cry,' said Rita. 'Everybody forgets things sometimes.'

'Mummy Annie's cross,' whispered Jason. 'She doesn't like me any more.'

'That's not true,' said Rita, struck by the pure misery on the little boy's face. 'She's just rushing about. People get snappy when they're pushed for time. Come on, have some breakfast.' She pushed the cereal packets across the table towards him, but Jason shook his head.

'No cereal?' said Rita, surprised. Jason loved his breakfast usually. 'Well, toast'll be ready soon.'

'Can't,' said Jason. He hung his head.

Charlie was digging his hands into the mush

again. Rita took them out and wiped them with the flannel. Still Jason looked down at his lap.

'Aren't you going to eat anything, Jason?' asked Rita. Gran swore by breakfast. She said you fainted, or got ill, if you skipped that first meal of the day. Rita didn't know what to do. 'Just one piece of toast, eh? With lots of jam,' she added desperately. 'You like jam, don't you?'

'I'm not allowed to. Naughty boys don't deserve to eat,' said Jason.

He sobbed, once. It was an awful sound, strangled in mid flow. Rita understood, instinctively, that Jason was afraid to cry aloud. Annie had said his life was awful before he came to them. Did that include being starved for forgetfulness and beaten for crying? As Jason looked up at her, she saw that was exactly it. The little frightened face tore her in two.

Where was everybody? A whole house full of people who would know what to say, and none of them here to help. Feeling completely crushed, Rita moved round to the little boy and cuddled him. 'No, you've got it wrong,' she said. 'It's different here. You're not a naughty boy, and even if you were, you could still have food and Mummy Annie would still love you.' Jason put his arms round her neck and sobbed again. Looking up, Rita saw Jody frozen in the doorway. She had heard every word. Rita felt stupid. But it had seemed like the right thing to say.

Jody disappeared. Suddenly Annie was there, her hands wet and tears in her eyes, taking Jason from Rita and cradling him on her lap. Jody must have fetched her.

'He said he didn't deserve breakfast . . . ' Rita started. Then she felt tears coming into her own eyes, and went to lock herself in the loo for a couple of minutes. By the time she felt recovered enough to come out, Annie and Jason were tucking into breakfast together and Jody was leaving the room with a piece of buttered toast in her hand. Slowly, Rita sat down at the table and spilled cornflakes into a bowl. Annie smiled at her. 'It's all right,' she mouthed, and indicated Jason, who was quite happily eating. Aloud, she said, 'We've got to go soon. I'm going to give Adam his bottle now. If Pete comes down, will you ask him to change Charlie? He smells awful.'

Rita nodded, and Annie left, cereal bowl in hand. Adam's frantic cries stopped suddenly, like a radio going dead in a power cut. Rita smiled as she imagined the bottle going into his mouth, like a plug. Finishing her cereal, and passing on the message to Pete who appeared just as she finished ('It's like Waterloo Station in here on school mornings,' he moaned), Rita took her bowl out to the kitchen. Jody was there, toast wedged between her teeth, ironing Jason's wet shorts. Steam rose and spat outwards. She flinched as the hot spray caught the back of her hand, and muttered what Rita thought to be a swear word through the toast.

'Are you all right?' Rita asked.

Jody nodded. She rested the iron on its stand, and laid the shorts on the back of the chair, where a sports shirt already lay. 'It's not going to come much drier than that,' she said. 'He'll have to wear it damp, if he can't face explaining to his teacher.' She looked at Rita with a faint but recognizable expression of approval. 'You were very good with him, for someone who doesn't have little kids around.'

'Thanks. It was so awful. I just said the first thing that came into my head, really. How could anyone stop feeding a little boy, or wallop him for crying? It's so cruel!'

Jody shrugged. 'We've had worse,' she said.

Rita couldn't imagine worse. Her gran was considered strict by all of Rita's friends. Rita sometimes felt suffocated and imprisoned by her gran's opinions and instructions: do this, do that, think this, say that. But Gran would never hit a child; perhaps a smack on the arm to show that when she said 'no' she had meant it, but not a real hit. She would say you had no right to pick on someone who was not your own size and who couldn't fight back, be it child or man. Rita could even hear her saying it.

Yet there were children everywhere, all over the world, perhaps even in this road, who were frightened of the very people who were supposed to love and care for them. It was a horrible thought, and one which made Rita despise herself for feeling miserable about being away from home. She didn't have *so* much to put up with. She was a whiner, as well as being plain, boring and awkward.

The chaos in the house reached its peak two minutes before Rita and Annie were due to leave for Rita's school. Everybody seemed to be frantic: Mark and Jody were arguing, Adam was crying, Charlie was running around with a bare bottom being chased by Jason, and Gnasher was chasing Jason and getting in everyone's way. Pete was accusing all and sundry of having moved his car keys.

'That's it, we're going. They're all yours!' yelled Annie. She slammed the door and breathed a deep sigh of relief. 'Let's get out of here,' she grinned at Rita.

In the quiet of the car, Rita turned her attention to the day ahead. It would be a bit of an ordeal. Her friends would be full of questions, some of them quite embarrassing. But it would be good to see them again, and once she had put them straight about what was going on the fuss would die down. Wendy had said she would take Rita with her to the flat on Tuesday (Rita refused to think about the issue of contacting Kathleen) and she would be able to pick up some more stuff, perhaps tidy up a bit, get a few things for Gran in the hospital.

They drew up outside the school. Annie looked at her watch. 'Well that was easier than I thought. We're early – twenty minutes! Sorry.'

'That's all right,' said Rita. A trickle of pupils were moving through the school gates into the play-ground. 'It'll give me a chance to see my friends, if they get here a bit early.'

'Mmm. That reminds me.' Annie reached into her pocket. She drew out a white envelope and some pound coins. 'Dinner money,' she explained, putting the coins into Rita's hand. 'There should be enough for a week there – it's what I give Mark and Jody for their school cafeteria – but if you run out, let me know. And this letter is for your Headteacher – Mr Jones, isn't it?'

Rita nodded, confused.

'It's just to explain what's going on,' said Annie.

'They have to keep the records up to date in case of accidents, and the school will need to know where you are living, and that there might be problems to sort out.'

'I don't need a letter,' said Rita. 'I can explain, if I need to.'

Annie smiled. 'I wish it were that simple. The school has to know, Rita. It'll be easier for you, for one thing. You'll see.'

Rita took the letter. She had not even considered the possibility that the school would be dragged into her family strife. She would be discussed at a staff meeting, she supposed, along with Tiger Bates who was always being suspended, and Janice Marlowe who was a known troublemaker throughout the school. Rita would be next on the agenda, and they'd all shake their heads and say how sad it was, poor Rita, and they'd better go easy on her for a while. The thought of all those sympathetic glances, careful questions and 'understanding' about homework made her feel sick.

'Are you going to be all right, Rita? You look a bit lost.'

Rita swung her hair onto her face. 'No, I'm fine. 'Bye.' She got out of the car in a hurry, dropping her bag in the gutter. At the school gate, she looked around. Annie's car was still there. Annie couldn't decide whether to follow her or not. Rita pushed back her hair, forced a smile, and waved. Annie waved back, relieved, and pulled off.

When the car was out of sight, Rita slipped back through the school gates and made off down the street. There was no way she could face school today.

The town centre was only five minutes walk from the school, but Rita deliberately took a longer route which would keep her off the main roads. She didn't want to be spotted by someone she knew. Once in the bustling shopping centre, mingling with early shoppers and people on their way to work, she felt less conspicuous, particularly as her school had a plain, dark uniform. She could easily be from one of the private schools, having a different half-term – or even someone who had left school, although she was sensible enough to know that if anything she looked a bit younger than her thirteen years, not older.

The question was, what could she do now? The whole day stretched out before her. She would have to be back at the school gates at three-thirty – not too early, because she would be noticed from the school windows, and not too late, because Annie would see her coming from another direction. She had to be there just as the crowd of children came out, so she could lose herself. Even then, one of her own friends or teachers might see her. And what about an absence note, when she did go back? Only now did Rita realize how complicated it would all be.

Rita looked at the clock above the jeweller's shop. There was just time to make it back to school before the first lesson. But no, she just couldn't face it. Everything was squeezing up inside her: worries about Gran; fears that Wendy might find Kathleen and bring her home; disgust with herself for being a thief and a liar; feeling ugly and babyish next to Jody – all this and much more, whizzing round her head and growing ever more tangled together, like a mass of seaweed in a stormy tide. Rita felt as if just one wrong remark, one strange look or sympathetic question, would open a huge floodgate, and it would all come out. She couldn't risk that.

Aimlessly she wandered around the shops. In her pocket she still had a little money from the five pounds Pete had given her, as well as the dinner money from Annie, but there was nothing she wanted to buy. Her head felt a bit fuzzy, as though a curtain had been pulled across her brain, and she didn't know where she was going or what to do when she got there. She simply walked: down the High Street, up Market Hill and around the market, left into one of the shopping arcades, right into the High Street again, left into another arcade, and so on. By the time Rita had walked all the way round the centre her legs were beginning to ache, and it was still only ten o'clock. She bought a can of drink and sat on one of the benches by a little green area, once pretty with bright flower beds but now covered in litter and the evidence of vandalism.

Sipping at her drink, Rita watched the people going by. Rush hour was over now, and the shoppers seemed to be more relaxed. A woman pushing a baby in a pram smiled at Rita as she sat down next to her to unwrap a bar of chocolate for the little boy who was walking at her side, looking already fed up with his expedition and ready to cause trouble.

Rita wondered whether Kathleen was still living in the same town. Not for the first time, she scanned the women passing by for a likeness to herself or Gran. It had always made her feel very strange to know that her own mother could pass her by in the street, serve her in a shop, even teach her at school, and Rita wouldn't know.

No matter how hard she tried not to play the stupid game, Rita couldn't stop herself, whenever she was in a crowd. Kathleen would now be in her late thirties; she could even be this woman sitting next to her.

A surge of rage filled Rita when she went over what Wendy had said. If it was true, that Gran had known where Kathleen was all these years and had even talked to her, it was unforgivable. How could Gran have brought Rita up with a secret like that hidden away? No photographs, no news, no mention even of her name. Gran had behaved as though Kathleen had never existed, a slate wiped clean. Rita had taken Kathleen's place in Gran's life, and she had needed no-one else. So when had Kathleen first contacted Gran, and what had they said? Whose idea was it to keep Rita in the dark? That was a very important question to have answered, and yet any answer would be unbearable. Either Kathleen didn't want any contact with her own daughter, which made Rita feel ten times more gawky and unlovable than a dozen Jodys could ever make her, or Kathleen wanted to see her and was blocked by Gran. (This, she had to admit, was not a very realistic option. After all, there would be nothing to stop Kathleen waiting outside the flat, or meeting Rita at school, if she really wanted to see her.)

The tangle grew and grew, and Rita began to feel agitated. She felt the same physical sensations as she did when she had been frightened by something: cold, clammy, a bit sick and wobbly but also desperate to *do* something. With a great surge of energy she jumped up from the bench and half-ran into the large department store on the other side of the square.

A wave of warm air and perfume hit her at the door. The make-up assistants, languishing at their counters, gave her barely more than a glance. No chance of a sale there. Rita lingered at the perfumes, trying one or two of the testers, but a baleful stare from a very elegant-looking assistant moved her on.

Next was the jewellery counter. Row upon row of earrings, bracelets, scarf pins, brooches and hair clips were arranged on little stands on the counters. Rita had no jewellery, except a small cross and chain that Gran had given her for her birthday. She was fascinated by the tiny, dainty earrings, dangling colours and shapes that swayed gently when she picked them up. The assistant had her back to Rita. She was talking to a man who wanted to buy something for his wife. Rita held some earrings up to her ears. They made her look very grown-up, she thought, as she caught her reflection in the little mirror. Maybe she should have her ears pierced. Gran would hit the roof. But it would serve Gran right. It would also serve Gran right if Rita *did* turn into a common thief. She imagined the shame Gran would feel, having people know that her grand-daughter had been stealing. What if Rita was caught thieving, and Gran had to come down to the police station to get her? She would never, ever get over it.

Rita's shame when she remembered that Gran would of course be far too ill to come to any police station, and was even now lying in a hospital bed, was only short-lived. It was soon replaced by a great rage that her grandmother's stroke had left Rita undefended, unprotected, plucked from her home and forced to live with strangers. Why hadn't Gran thought about what would happen if she got ill? Why hadn't she insisted on Kathleen coming to visit her child, so that in the event of an emergency there was something she could do? Gran hadn't cared about Rita at all.

The assistant was still talking to the man. They laughed together. Rita put two pairs of earrings into her pocket. She didn't even look round first, she just slipped them in. She waited for a shout, for a hand on her shoulder, but none came. Next she took a bangle, putting it onto her wrist as if to try it on, and then picking up another one. She only replaced one, and moved down the counter looking intently at other things. The bangle was edged up under her jumper.

It was so easy. She grew bolder. Another pair of earrings, and a brooch, found their way into her pockets. This time she did look around. Surely someone had spotted her. But everyone was busy with their own purchases. The make-up girls were talking to each other, paying no attention to what was going on around them.

'Can I help you?' The assistant had finally noticed her. Rita felt hot. She was sure the girl would notice the bulge under her jumper where the bangle lay around her wrist.

'No – just looking,' she said.

'OK,' smiled the girl. But having no-one else to serve, she busied herself with the little displays, casting a glance over in Rita's direction now and then. Half of Rita wanted to try and steal right from under her nose, but that was the half that didn't care about being caught, or perhaps even wanted to. The other half, the sensible half that was horrified at what she was doing, won out. Rita moved on.

By the time she was ready to leave the department store Rita's pockets were almost full. She had taken jewellery, sweets, even two tiny teddies, although the toy department staff were more vigilant. No-one had challenged her; indeed, she had been smiled at, chatted to, by several assistants who had seen a small, rather sad-looking little thing and responded with the warmth of those who want to take every lost puppy home with them. None of them had suspected they were helping a thief. Long years of covering up her true feelings so as not to 'make an exhibition of herself' (Gran's constant horror) meant there was no sign on her face of the churning stomach, the wobbly legs, the terror of being completely mad and out of control that Rita actually felt.

She left the store almost in a dream. Once outside, she headed for the public conveniences and locked herself inside a loo. There, she was sick. Then she transferred the stolen goods from her pocket to her school bag.

Rita sat down on the seat of the loo and leaned back against the cistern pipes. What on earth was she doing? Rita had read about people who stole things from shops when they were under stress. Mrs Stokey, one of Gran's friends, had been apprehended by the manager of the local supermarket after walking out with three tins of cat food under her coat. Mrs Stokey didn't even have a cat.

Gran had said Mrs Stokey didn't know what she was doing. It happened sometimes, Gran said, and didn't mean people were off their trolleys, just unhappy. Mrs Stokey's husband had run off with the decorator from the council who had been doing up their flat.

Rita was certainly unhappy. But what could she do? She badly needed to talk to Gran, explain what was happening. Gran would understand. She had not shunned Mrs Stokey, as Rita had expected her to after the incident, but had continued to invite her in for tea and to watch the wrestling on Saturday afternoons. Gradually the other members of Gran's clan, who had been shocked at Gran's insistence on keeping her friendship with Mrs Stokey, had filtered back, and the whole thing was forgotten. But only Gran could help Rita, because only Gran would know that Rita was not a thief by nature. If Annie and Pete found out, they would not want her in the house. She would be talked about at school, and the teachers wouldn't trust her. Gran was too sick to help Rita sort this mess out, and without her Rita felt completely swamped. She hadn't the faintest idea what to do next.

7

'How did you get on?' asked Annie anxiously.

'OK,' said Rita. Her tone did not invite further questioning.

Back at the Browns' house, there was an unusual air of calm. Annie explained that her mother had taken the two little ones to meet Jason and then go on to the park. Jody and Mark were both at friends' houses, and Pete had gone to work early because he was going to stop off somewhere on the way.

'So it's just you and me,' smiled Annie. 'Do you want to talk?'

'About what?' asked Rita, her heart pounding. Perhaps Annie knew: someone must have seen Rita in town. Or perhaps Wendy phoned the school, and they told her Rita Dennison wasn't there. It would be a relief, to be forced to tell. But she didn't want to end up in a children's home or some other institution, and she was sure that would happen if Annie knew the truth.

'We can talk about anything you like,' smiled Annie. 'But I did wonder if you were clear about what's going on – with your gran and so on – and whether there was anything you wanted to ask, or anything you'd like Pete or me to do.'

'Oh.'

'Is there anything you want to talk about, Rita?'

'No, I don't think so.' She waited for Annie to push the point, but Annie just smiled again and said, 'Well, in that case, I would take advantage of the peace and quiet if I were you. Chaos will return soon enough. Do you have homework?'

'Homework? I don't think so – I mean, no. They never give us any on the first day.'

'Very civil. What do you want to do, then? Fancy coming over to the park to meet Mum and the little ones?'

'No thanks. Do you mind if I watch television?'

'Of course not. This is your home for the time being, Rita. You don't have to ask permission.'

'Sorry.'

'No, it's all right, don't apologize. Listen, we're having dinner about six, and then I'll nip you over to the hospital to see your gran.'

'No!' snapped Rita. The last thing she needed was the sight of her gran lying helpless, knowing that she wouldn't be able to say the things she needed to say to her. Rita was scared of the rage that was still festering in her. She might lose control.

Annie was looking at her strangely. 'I didn't mean to snap,' said Rita. 'I'm really tired, and feel a bit headachey. Gran needs her rest and anyway, I'll be going tomorrow with Wendy. Gran will be all right for just one night without seeing me.'

'It's up to you, of course. But I'm sure your gran will be pleased to see you. Are you sure, Rita?'

Rita nodded, and Annie sighed. This child was heavy going. She didn't envy Wendy the task of trying to sort out what was going on inside that head. But Annie wasn't going to push the point. She wasn't so desperate to turn out after dinner and drive across town to wait in the car park and drive back. 'Will you be all right on your own, if I go and meet Mum?'

All right? It would be bliss. 'Yes, I'll be fine,' said Rita. ''Bye.'

Once alone she climbed the stairs and pulled out the drawer on her bed. The bubble bath lay accusingly where she had put it. Quickly she added the things she had taken from the department store.

'This has got to stop!' she told herself aloud, through gritted teeth.

But she didn't know how to stop. Perhaps Jody or Annie would find the things in the drawer, and ask questions. Rita didn't want this to happen, but still she closed the drawer rather carelessly, so that it didn't quite shut. Then she lay on her bed, staring up at the ceiling and trying to work out what to do next. Tomorrow she would have to decide what to do about school, and she would have to go and see Gran, and Wendy would be asking awkward questions about Kathleen. It was all too much. The more she tried to work out a plan, the more confused she became.

When she heard a key in the front door below, Rita ran silently up the stairs and turned on the television. Somehow, she managed to get through the evening meal without drawing attention to herself. Annie was busy with Adam, Jody and Mark were bantering as usual and Jason was full of news about his day at school. After dinner Jody washed up, Mark bathed Charlie and Rita disappeared upstairs again to pretend to watch television. Later she was joined by Mark, but he only asked her how school had been and what she was watching. After that he settled down to watch the film. Jody went out somewhere; when Rita went to bed, she was still not home. Rita was very relieved about this. Jody was not busy like Annie, or prepared to accept what she saw on the surface, like Mark. Jody was sharp. She noticed things, asked questions, and made Rita wriggle inside. All Rita wanted to do was sleep.

She did sleep, all night. Her sleep was deep and dreamless, undisturbed even by Jody crashing about when she came to bed (in a bad temper, as Rita learned from Mark the following day, because Annie had been cross with her for staying out later than agreed). But when Jody's alarm went off the next morning Rita woke feeling just as tired as she had the night before. It was a real effort to get up. What she wanted to do, more than anything, was go back under the covers and stay there. The day ahead held no attraction whatsoever.

The chaos at breakfast was much the same as the day before. Then Rosie arrived to help out, as Pete was still at work. She took charge, as usual, and everything seemed to fall into place.

'I'll be back as quick as I can, Mum,' said Annie. 'When you take Jason to school, can you remind him to give in his dinner money? He forgot yesterday. It's in his bag.'

'Yes, I will. And you watch what you're doing on those roads,' said Rosie sternly. 'I'd rather be late up at the club than be visiting you in hospital somewhere.'

'Oh Mum!' Annie kissed her on the cheek and picked up her car keys. 'Ready, Rita?'

Rita, who had no intention of going to school, nodded and clutched her school bag. There was nothing inside it except her purse and a packet of tissues.

'You look tired,' said Rosie, looking closely at Rita. 'And your hair's all in tangles. Where's your brush?'

From anyone else, Rita would have taken offence at what she considered to be such a personal remark. But to Rosie she was just another child, and Rita did not mind being mothered a bit. 'I haven't got one,' she said. 'I left it at home. I've been using a comb, but – '

'You should have said,' Annie cut in. 'You could have borrowed a brush. Here,' she took one from the little table in the hall, 'use Jody's. She won't mind.'

'Mind what?' Jody was on the first landing.

'Can Rita use your brush?' asked Rosie. 'She's left hers at the flat.'

'Sure. Actually, you can keep it. I've got at least two more somewhere around the place.'

'Thank you,' muttered Rita. She didn't want Jody's charity, and she was embarrassed.

'Come on, you can do your hair in the car. We don't want to be late. 'Bye, everybody.'

Gnasher, who had flopped his eleven-stone bulk across the front door, looked up at Annie with sorrowful eyes as she nudged him with her foot, but he didn't move. It was impossible to get past him. 'Get up, Gnasher!' shouted Annie in frustration. 'You're not coming. You'll get your walk later.'

Mark popped his head round the dining room door and laughed. 'He's at it again, is he?'

'At what?' asked Rita.

'He didn't get his walk last night,' explained Annie. 'He was forgotten. This is his protest. He knows full well we can't get out of the house without using this door, and he knows I can't move him. I think the idea is that we'll let him come with us. You're a real pain, Gnasher. *Get up!!*'

Gnasher didn't move.

'On your marks!' shouted Mark suddenly. As if familiar with the signal, Jody came down the stairs, Rosie stepped back out of the way, taking Rita by the arm, and Annie clutched the door latch.

'Get set!' Mark grabbed Gnasher's collar and Jody placed her hands on his haunches. Gnasher made a half-hearted move to snap at Mark's hand, but no-one seemed to feel there was any danger of him actually following it through.

'Go!'

Rita watched in amazement as Mark heaved and Jody pushed Gnasher's unyielding body. After a moment he scrambled to his feet, though still refusing to move. Jody continued to push, while Mark took a firm grip on Gnasher's collar and dragged him towards the kitchen. As soon as the door could be opened a little way, Annie beckoned Rita and they squeezed through. Gnasher, once clear of the door, put all his energies to jumping up and trying to follow them. Rosie slammed the door just in time. Annie and Rita, safely outside, heard him bark in frustration.

'The real fun will come when Mum wants to

leave the house with a double buggy and Jason,' grinned Annie.

'What will she do?'

'Oh, she'll be all right. Usually she entices him into the kitchen with something to eat and shuts the door on him. Gnasher may be big and strong, but he's pretty stupid. He usually falls for it.'

'Can't you train him to – ?'

'Train Gnasher?' Annie laughed. 'Believe me, we've tried. The trouble is, we got him from a family who couldn't cope with him. By the time they found a home – us – Gnasher was more or less running the show. He'll obey Pete, most of the time, but he treats the rest of us with the contempt he feels we deserve. He would never hurt anyone; he's always gentle, even with the little ones who pull him around and try to dress him up and things. But if he doesn't want to do something, he won't. That's that.'

'Did you not have Gnasher from a puppy, then?' asked Rita in the car.

'No. He was already three years old.'

'A foster dog,' smiled Rita. Trust the Browns to have even their pet second-hand.

'Exactly. We agreed to have him for a couple of weeks to give the family a breather. Then they said they didn't want him back, and he'd have to be put down. Well, you can imagine how Jody and Mark felt about that. So there we were, lumbered.'

'He is lovely, though,' said Rita.

'So are polar bears, but I wouldn't want to live with one,' said Annie grimly. 'Personally, I would prefer a poodle.'

Rita couldn't work out whether she was joking or not.

They reached the school a little later than the previous day. Rita dived into the crowds, praying that she would not be seen by anyone from her class. She was spotted by one or two people who knew her vaguely, but no-one in her close circle. She hung around in the playground until she was sure Annie would be gone, and then slipped out.

'You're going the wrong way!' said a sixth former as she passed him on the street.

'Forgot something,' said Rita breathlessly.

'Have a good time in late detention then,' he grinned.

Rita knew him by sight, but she was sure he wouldn't know her name or even remember that he'd seen her, if asked. So once more she reached the town centre unspotted. She wandered into one store after another, sizing up how good the security was, and then went back to ones where she felt there was little risk of being caught. There was none of the previous day's guilt and soul-searching; Rita was out to enjoy herself. It was exciting, to pit her wits against the store's security. It made her feel clever, and daring – more like the Rita she had left behind at the flat, and less like the little wimp staying in the Browns' house.

Once she accepted that she had become a thief, there was no point in worrying about it. 'In for a penny, in for a pound,' as Gran would say. And it would serve Gran right to be known as the grand-mother of a thief, pay her back for keeping in touch with Kathleen behind Rita's back.

Rita decided from the start that she would not

steal anything that could be of any use to her, or anything she really liked and wanted for herself. It became part of the game, to choose the most unsuitable or useless target, and then steal it. During the course of the day she stole a sociology textbook, two pairs of men's socks, a cigarette lighter and some impossibly large women's underwear. She would not have dreamed of taking anything that she herself would want to use. If caught – *when* caught, for she knew it was inevitable, she didn't want anyone to think she had done it from greed.

Every time she walked out of a shop and wasn't stopped, Rita felt more powerful. She used her school dinner money to buy a burger and a drink without any qualm of conscience at all, and sailed back to the school gate at exactly the right moment to meet Annie, feeling invincible and on top of the world. It was like being a bit drunk, and it was a wonderful feeling.

It didn't last. Once inside the car, with Annie asking her about her day and her bag heavy with useless stolen goods, Rita began to look more sensibly at what she had done. She was disgusted with herself. How could she let Gran down like that? If only she had been caught that very first time, in the hospital shop. She wished now that the woman had seen her taking the bubble bath and escorted her back to the Browns with an indignant demand for payment. Then they wouldn't have trusted her. They would perhaps have checked with the school, watched her more carefully. But Annie was chatting away as though Rita was one of the clan. What would she say if she knew the truth?

Suddenly Rita didn't want to be caught. All day she had been half-hoping, without even realizing it fully, that someone would stop her. But now she became terrified that she *had* been seen, and that there would be someone at the house, or coming to the school, to arrest her. I'll never do it again, she told herself. Never. It was stupid, stupid and mad. Whatever happens, I'll never steal again.

This promise to herself didn't make the bad feelings go away, nor did it help to see Wendy's car outside the house when they got back to the Browns'.

'Wendy's going to take you back to the flat to get some stuff together, and then on to the hospital,' said Annie. 'Is that all right?'

Rita, knowing that she could not get away with another refusal to go to the hospital without some very searching questions, nodded.

'Do you want a cup of tea and a sandwich first?'

'No – I'll just take my bag upstairs,' said Rita. She skirted round Gnasher, who was wagging his tail in greeting, and ran up to Jody's room. When she came down, Wendy was sitting in the living room holding Adam and talking to Pete. The conversation stopped as Rita appeared, her school bag and its hidden secrets stowed away in the drawer.

'Hello, Rita,' said Wendy. Her smile was a little wary. 'How are you?'

'OK.' Rita tried not to scowl.

'Good. Um, Annie tells me you didn't want to go and see your gran yesterday.'

Rita didn't answer.

'I looked in on her last night, Rita,' said Pete gently. 'She's a lot better – asked for you, in fact.'

Rita looked at him in disbelief, but he met her eyes steadily. 'She really is a lot better, Rita.'

'So, are you going to see her tonight?' asked Wendy.

Rita shrugged. 'Suppose so.'

'Well look. I have to be at a meeting later on, but I thought I'd take you to the flat and then on to the hospital. I wouldn't come up to the ward, though. Annie says she can collect you in the car, if you call when you're ready. How would that be?'

'All right,' said Rita flatly.

'Fine,' sighed Wendy. 'Come on then. I'll stand you a burger or something after we've been to the flat, so that you don't starve.'

As she followed Rita out of the room, Wendy looked at Pete and raised her eyebrows. He shook his head slightly. They had been hoping to give Rita a piece of news, but both felt instinctively that more ground had to be prepared before they let Rita know that the hospital had found Kathleen. She was a long way away, in Scotland. But she had told the hospital that she would try and visit her mother at the end of the week.

Like it or not, by the weekend Rita would almost certainly be coming face to face with the mother who was a complete stranger to her.

8

'How have you settled in, Rita? Are you OK with the Browns?' Please say yes, Wendy added mentally. I've got two more appointments after you and if you add even more to my workload I'll scream.

'It's all right,' said Rita.

'Mmm. Getting on all right with Jody?'

Rita shrugged. Then she said 'Yes, I suppose so.'

'Jody can be a bit insensitive sometimes, but she's a good kid at heart. I've got to know the Browns quite well over the last couple of years and I think they're lovely. What about that dog! More like a small horse, isn't he?'

'Yes.' Rita turned her head to look out of the window. She didn't want to chat. She wished Wendy would stop talking and drive.

Wendy sighed. There was clearly something troubling the girl, something she needed to talk about. But how to unlock all those doors Rita had closed on herself? Even if she did talk, there was no guarantee Wendy would be able to help. She was already running herself ragged trying to keep up with the work she had. Any extra and she'd more likely go and shoot herself than be any real help to anyone! So, although part of her wanted to push

Rita for more information, the tired part of her didn't want to hear any more problems. She turned up the radio. 'I hope you like music.'

'Yes,' said Rita.

The music was a classical piece Rita had heard somewhere before, perhaps in school assembly. It was quite famous, but she couldn't remember the name of it. It was pleasant enough, the kind of music that washed over you without stirring you up inside. Rita watched the drivers of other cars as they edged past in the right-hand filter lane at the traffic lights queue. Some were singing along to tapes or radio; some were engaged in animated conversation with a passenger. One man was eating a sandwich, another was reading a map propped up against the wheel. In one car a woman was applying make-up. Every time the car stopped in the traffic she would pull out a little mirror and some mascara from somewhere, flinging them down when the traffic moved again. Rita had never noticed how unstill people in cars were. She was the only one who was just sitting. Even Wendy was tapping out a rhythm on the steering wheel with her hands.

To keep her mind busy, so that she wouldn't think about what she was going to say to Gran, Rita tried to count the number of times she had been in a car before Gran's stroke. Almost never: possibly she had done more car journeys in the last few days than she had done in the whole of the previous year. She had been on coaches and buses of course, but not cars; she and Gran didn't know many people who owned one. When she had recalled the few lifts home from friends' parents and an occasional outing with them, Rita turned to making a mental list of what she would need from the flat. She was looking forward to seeing her home again. She hoped it wasn't too messy. They had left in such a rush, with the ambulance flashing its blue light urgently outside, that Rita had had no time to think about tidying up.

The flat was spotless. Everything was neat and scrubbed. One of Gran's friends in the block had a key, Rita remembered. She must have come in and cleaned it. This did not surprise Rita. The estate they lived on was a friendly one, and in their block everyone chipped in to help when there was a crisis: Rita had seen it happen before, to others. Gran was always a part of things. She should have realized the same supports would be there for her and Gran, too.

What did surprise Rita was the size of the place. It had always seemed perfectly adequate but now it looked tiny, and cramped. Already she was used to the high ceilings, the light-coloured walls and the space of the Browns' house. Now her own home looked shabby, crammed with fussy ornaments and things which didn't match. Rita didn't mind the difference; this was her home and it could never look anything but good to *her*. But it was a shock to see it as Wendy must be seeing it, to compare it – as Wendy no doubt would – to what they had just left.

'Gran likes to have things around her,' said Rita. 'We always mean to have a clear-out, but the things are too precious to get rid of.'

Wendy smiled. 'I know exactly what you mean. I'm the same. This looks lovely and homely.'

'It is. We like it, anyway,' said Rita. She didn't know why she still felt defensive, even after Wendy had said how nice it was. 'Would you like a cup of tea?'

Wendy hesitated, and looked a bit awkward. 'I'd love one, Rita, but the thing is I'm running awfully late. Do you mind terribly if we just get your stuff and move on? Hopefully you'll be able to come back for a longer visit some other time; we'll ask Annie about buses if you like, see if there's one from their house over to this part of town. I am sorry.'

'It's all right,' said Rita. She was disappointed. She wanted to show Wendy how well she and Gran managed. They always made visitors feel welcome, too, just like the Browns, but a bit more formal. The best china lay waiting, and there was always a shop-bought fruit cake in the cupboard in case Gran didn't have time to bake one. A neighbour would have provided the milk, and Wendy would have seen how easy it would be for Gran to come home when she was a bit better. But Wendy was in a hurry, and Rita didn't have time to sit a while and absorb the atmosphere of home again, before she would start to forget it.

Rita went into the bedroom and piled a few clothes into a suitcase. Wendy followed her.

'You share the bedroom?' she asked, surprised.

'Yes. Why shouldn't we?'

'No reason. I just thought these flats looked bigger from the outside, that's all. I didn't mean any offence, Rita.'

Rita turned away. She packed everything she thought she might need for a week or so, accepting Wendy's assurance that she would be able to come back, and picked up a few things for Gran. Wendy waited in the lounge.

'Here.' Rita came into the room very slowly with her case. She held out a small cloth-bound book to Wendy. 'I found it in Gran's personal things. If she knows Kathleen's telephone number, it will be in there somewhere. So there's no need for you to go through Gran's things. She wouldn't want you to, not even to find Kathleen. Here, take it.'

Wendy reached out her hand and took the book from Rita, but she laid it unopened on the small table at her side. 'Sit down a minute, Rita. There's something I need to tell you. We don't need this little book – the hospital spoke to your mum last night on the telephone.'

'Spoke to who?' asked Rita. She was playing for time, pretending that the word 'mum' meant nothing to her. Her heart started to pound a rhythm into her ears.

'Kathleen,' said Wendy. 'Your real mother. One of your gran's neighbours contacted her, and she phoned the hospital. She's coming down from Scotland later in the week. I'm sorry, Rita, to land it on you like this but there's no easy way.'

Wendy moved across to sit beside Rita on the sofa, but Rita moved away from the arm that tried to embrace her.

'Why? Why did they have to do that? You said Gran was getting better . . . '

'She is, she is,' Wendy hastily assured her. 'It's just the done thing to let the next of kin know when someone's ill like this.'

'*I'm* the next of kin. *Me*, not her! We don't need her, Gran and me. Tell her to stay where she is.'

92

Rita felt as if her whole body was being ripped into little pieces. It was a nightmare. War raged inside her: one side wanted to know everything about Kathleen, longed to see her at last; the other side knew that life could never be the same if Kathleen surfaced from the deep dark of history and took on human flesh. But whatever was going to happen, Rita, the one person whose life was being totally torn apart, would have no say. It was out of her control. They, whoever the faceless 'they' happened to be in this case, would map out Rita's life and expect her to live it. No questions, no explanations. A life without a mother, and then a life with one, just like that.

'I can't stop her from coming,' said Wendy gently. 'It's her mother lying in hospital, and you're still her daughter . . . '

'No, I'm not. I don't have a mother.' Rita's voice was flat. She was not going to fight. Why bother? They would win in the end. Whatever *they* wanted her to do, she would have to do it. That was what being a child was all about. You had no power, no choices, unless you made the choices *they* wanted you to. Well, she would give in graciously. She hadn't the strength for anything else.

'You don't have to see your . . . Kathleen, you know, if you really don't want to.' Wendy put her hand on Rita's shoulder. 'We can talk about it tomorrow. We'll decide what to do then, when the shock's worn off a bit, eh?'

Rita shrugged, and hung her head. Wendy moved closer, and this time Rita submitted to a small, stiff hug. It was not as good as the way Rosie hugged,

93

making her feel safe and strong, but it showed that Wendy understood a bit.

Wendy looked at her watch with a sinking heart. Next on the list was an elderly woman whose constant demands and strange behaviour were proving too much for the son with whom she lived. Wendy was afraid the son, who had been ill himself for some years, was going to snap soon. He was counting on Wendy's visits for a bit of sane company and reassurance that he could cope. Wendy had said she would be there by now. She couldn't miss the visit, and that would make her late for the foster parents' support group she was supposed to be chairing. These days were becoming all too common. Yet another snatched burger eaten in the car on the way to somewhere, yet another skimped visit without doing a thorough job. She just hoped she could make it through to the following week, when she had some leave booked.

'We'd better get going,' she said to Rita. 'We can talk in the car.'

Rita refused to talk, however. All Wendy's attempts to draw her out met with shrugs or grunts, or bare one-word answers. They were both relieved when they stopped at the take-away burger place and had food to concentrate on.

When the car drew up outside the hospital, Wendy said, 'Do you want me to come in with you? I will, if you need me to.'

Rita shook her head. 'I'll be all right – honestly. I'll telephone Annie when I need a lift. Thanks.' She got out of the car and walked into the main entrance, knowing that Wendy was watching her. As she made the journey down the long corridors and up the stairs towards Evelyn Ward, Rita's pace got slower and slower. She wanted to see Gran, whose absence left a gaping hole in her life, but she didn't know what she was going to say when she saw her. She wanted to snuggle up and sob her heart out, to feel Gran's thin hand patting her on the shoulder and hear her saying 'There, there, it'll come right in the end.' But she wanted to shake her, too, until her bones rattled. The violence she felt frightened her.

In the end she stood outside the ward for some time, gathering the courage to go in. Gran was looking better. She was propped up on her pillows, and she recognized Rita. Her smile of greeting swept away Rita's anger. 'You're better!' she whooped, and gave her gran a fierce hug and kiss on the cheek.

'Ree-tah!' said Gran. Her voice was strange, still a bit growly, and she seemed to search very carefully for the few words she could say. But she was alert, and able to listen. Rita told her about the Browns, with all their children and their huge dog. She told her about the flat being all spruced up. Gran nodded, understanding at least most of what was said. Occasionally she struggled to ask a question, and Rita tried to guess what it was she wanted to know. They even laughed together. Rita knew that she could forgive her gran anything, she was so thankful to see her like this. Rita had been sure, deep down, that Gran was going to die. Now all that insecurity was pushed aside. Soon Gran would be well enough to leave hospital, and come home. Rita would look after her; life would start again and Rita would bury the shame of what she had done and go back to normal. It was like having a great weight lifted from her shoulders.

Rita started to tell Gran about her plans for the future. She would take Gran on the bus to the park where the Browns had taken her. It was a lovely place, and Gran could sit in the sun and get strong again.

Gran suddenly gripped her hand. 'Ree-tah,' she said through her twisted mouth. 'See Kaythlin.'

'Gran, I can't understand you,' lied Rita. She wasn't ready to discuss Kathleen yet.

'Kaythlin. Kaythlin!' said Gran urgently. Her eyes were burning. She was looking over Rita's shoulder.

A cool, soft voice said, 'Hello, Rita.'

As if dreaming, Rita stood up and turned around. A well-dressed woman, who looked impossibly like Gran but much younger, smiled nervously at her. 'I'm Kathleen. I'm your mother.'

9

It was a moment that would haunt Rita all her life – the moment she first saw her mother. Her hands and feet turned to stone, and there was a swimming sound in her ears. She looked at Kathleen for a long time, and yet saw nothing. If you had asked Rita for a description of Kathleen at that moment, she would not have been able to supply it. Rita felt her body stiffen. A hot wave swept over her face, making her nose sweat. Then, just as suddenly, she went cold. She opened her mouth to say hello, but couldn't. Kathleen didn't move, and Gran didn't move. A nurse came towards the bed, smiling, and suddenly changed direction and went to the other side of the ward.

'Hello, Rita,' said Kathleen again. 'I bet you're surprised to see me, eh?'

It seemed such a stupid thing to say that Rita almost laughed, but it brought her back to reality. 'Hello, Kathleen,' she said.

Kathleen grimaced, as if hearing her daughter use her Christian name was strange, but surely she didn't expect Rita to call her Mum? Rita, unable to say more, looked at her mother and looked away. This time the image of Kathleen stayed in her mind as vividly as if she were still looking at her. Kathleen was tall and slim, dressed in very fashionable and expensive clothes. Her dark hair was cut into a shiny, shoulder length bob; not a hair out of place. Rita automatically put her hand to her own hair, which looked like a dark haystack as usual, and brushed it from her face, self-consciously.

'How are you?' asked Kathleen.

Rita didn't answer.

Kathleen shifted her feet. 'God, I'm dying for a cigarette. Look, come outside with me, Rita, eh?' Without waiting for an answer, Kathleen turned to Gran. 'I'm just going for a ciggy, Ma. All right? Back in a minute. Come on,' she said to Rita. And Rita followed her. Afterwards she could have kicked herself for following the command like a little lamb, but her legs seemed to do it automatically, without her brain having any involvement.

Outside the ward, in the corridor, Kathleen pulled out a packet of cigarettes. She offered one to Rita. Rita, scandalized, looked pointedly at the 'No Smoking' sign. Kathleen followed her eyes, and shrugged. She lit the cigarette. 'Very prim and proper, aren't you?' she said. 'I suppose I should have expected that, with you being with Mum all these years.' Her tone was one of friendly interest. She could just as easily have been talking about a chimpanzee at the zoo as her own flesh and blood. 'So, how have you been getting on?'

Did she mean now, with the Browns? Or was she referring to the thirteen years since she had left Rita in her mother's flat and taken a train out of their lives forever? It was impossible to ask, and impossible even to speak. Rita wouldn't know where to start; whether it should be with the anger she felt building up, the tears that were threatening to spill, or the question that hung in the air between them: why? Why leave me, why stay in touch with Gran and not with me? Why? Why? The question burned in her mind, like a huge spotlight bulb, flooding everything with such a powerful light that nothing except the question could be seen.

'Why?' She had actually said it.

Kathleen looked surprised. 'Why what?'

'Why do you want to know?'

Kathleen drew on her cigarette. Through a smoky haze, she looked at her daughter with narrowed eyes. 'I'm not sure,' she said. 'Perhaps it's because you're my kid, and I feel I ought to take an interest.'

'I'm not your kid,' said Rita bitterly.

'So whose are you then? That old biddy's in there? If not mine, Rita, whose?'

'No-one's.' It was true. Without Gran, she had no-one. Only herself.

'Well, anyway,' said Kathleen, drawing on her cigarette again.

In the silence that followed, Rita fought to keep herself from turning on her heel and running away. Kathleen seemed outwardly calm, though she flicked her cigarette constantly, even when there was no ash on the tip.

Rita had not expected hugs and kisses and long explanations, but she had expected something a bit more than this. There should at least have been some sign of guilt, some attempt to explain. She doesn't see the need to explain, thought Rita

99

angrily. I'm nothing to her, nothing at all. Why couldn't she just stay away?

'How long are you staying?' Rita asked aloud, trying not to sound too angry. She barely managed it; there was a fury building up inside that could erupt like a volcano at any moment.

'Not sure,' said Kathleen. She stared out of the small window high up in the corridor. Only a patch of grey sky was visible. 'It depends.'

'Oh?' Rita waited.

Kathleen turned, with an effort, to face her. 'How long do you want me to stay, Rita?'

Rita shrugged. 'I don't care,' she said. Actually, that wasn't true at all. She wanted her mother to get back on the first train to her own place, and never come near Rita again. She wished she could say that, but it was impossible. Jody, of course, would have said it. Rita could see the scornful flashing eyes now, daring Kathleen to say any more. But Rita did not have the courage.

'That's not much of an answer.' Kathleen gave a small, tight smile. 'I can see you're being polite, Rita. Nice manners – better than you'd have learned from me, I dare say.'

She ought to have been Jody's mum, not mine, thought Rita bitterly. Jody would have done this so much better than me.

Her mother was still watching her; it made Rita squirm. The anger was like a bubbling stew, lifting the lid of the pan and making it rattle. It would not be ignored; Rita had to let a little escape to stop the whole lot spilling over. She scuffed her heels on the shiny hospital floor. 'Look, why did you bother to come at all? You hate my gran, don't you? And to be honest, we never even think about you; you don't really exist as far as we're concerned. So why bother?'

Kathleen's cigarette froze halfway to her mouth, then was lowered. She looked at Rita through a small spiralling swirl of smoke, eyes half-narrowed. 'I've come because the hospital asked me to – said Mum might die, and was asking for me. I've come because I have just as much right as you to be here, and to say goodbye. I'm not pretending we got on. You're right – I hated her and she hated me, most of the time. But if she died, well, that would be different, wouldn't it?'

'How?'

'What?' Kathleen was startled by the question.

'How different?'

Kathleen tossed the stub of her cigarette onto the hospital floor and stepped on it, grinding it into the polish. She did not pick it up; it lay there, between her feet and Rita's. 'God, but you're a strange kid,' said Kathleen.

'What did you expect?'

Kathleen smiled nervously. 'Do you always talk in questions?'

'Do you ever give straight answers?' returned Rita.

Kathleen pulled her cigarettes out of her bag. She flicked the packet open, looked at Rita and closed it again. 'Look, I'm not very good at this sort of thing. Can we start again?'

Rita shrugged.

'Rita, I left you for a reason, you know. I had to do it. I didn't really want to. But there I was with a baby and no man – the skunk ran off soon as he knew about you – and everybody's tongues wagging. I wasn't getting any younger, I knew I had to make the break sometime. And Mum was going on and on about the disgrace, and never giving me time to think or breathe . . . every time I wanted her to look after you so I could have a bit of fun, it was like a major inconvenience. She made me feel like a tart. Compared to her, I suppose anyone would have been a tart. I don't know to this day how she managed to have me . . . ' Kathleen's voice tailed off. 'Well anyway, that's all water under the bridge now. The thing was, I wanted to take you with me, of course I did, but I didn't know where I was going, or when I would have a roof over my head. It wouldn't have been fair to any kiddy to live that sort of life . . . ' Again, she seemed to run out of steam.

The fact was, Kathleen didn't know what to say to the kid. She could understand Rita's anger, written plainly all over the stiff little face. After all, Kathleen had run off and left her, and no doubt Mum had poisoned the girl's mind. But it wasn't as if she was a bad person. She had left Rita with her gran, not abandoned her in a shop doorway. She had sent money now and then, when she could afford it, and she had called Mum sometimes to check they were OK. It would have done no good to come back into Rita's life once she was settled and had built a proper life of her own. Then there was Ken. She had never told him about Rita, not even when they got married. She'd tried to, but when they found they couldn't have children of their own, she had put it out of her mind. She could never tell Ken.

Rita had probably been happy enough. Happier than she would have been with Kathleen, anyway. Kathleen felt she had actually been quite noble and self-sacrificing when she left her baby behind and went off into the unknown.

For Rita, the situation was impossible. There was so much that she wanted to say that it all pushed against her until she could say absolutely nothing. The window in the corridor was open; they were three floors up. Rita wanted to push this woman out over the sill and into the street. She could picture the blood and brains spilling out all over the carefully cut suit, picture the twisted legs swelling in the spiky shoes. Kathleen would be gone, out of her life for ever. Rita and Gran would be left in peace. If only she had the courage and the strength to do it. But she couldn't. The urge was almost uncontrollable, and yet she couldn't.

There were footsteps in the corridor. Rita turned, and saw Pete walking towards her. His smile froze slightly when he saw her face, and his eyes shifted to Kathleen. His expression was strange; Rita couldn't work out what he thought. He moved alongside Rita and they faced Kathleen together. It didn't seem possible that he could know who this woman was, but he seemed to. 'Hi, Rita – I've come to collect you.' He smiled at Rita, and looked again at Kathleen. 'Hello,' he said, and his voice was different – cool, a bit wary. This could only be because he was worried for Rita, and she felt a part of her warming up again. Kathleen didn't care about Rita at all, but there were others who did.

Kathleen smiled and extended a hand. 'Well,

hello. I'm Rita's mother. Kathleen McDonald – used to be Dennison, before I married.'

This new information caught Rita by surprise, and she gasped. She felt Pete's hand on her arm. Steady, now, he seemed to be saying. Keep calm.

'Pleased to meet you,' he said stiffly. 'I'm Peter Brown. Rita is staying with my family for the time being.'

'Oh good,' said Kathleen vaguely. 'I'm so glad she didn't have to go into a children's home or something. Of course, I could look after her myself, now that I'm here . . . '

Pete felt Rita's arm stiffen, and gave it a squeeze. 'I think the social worker feels she's well settled with us,' he said. 'And we certainly like having her around. You have a beautiful daughter, Mrs McDonald, one to be proud of.'

Rita blushed, but felt warmth beginning to creep further into her body.

'Um, yes, well she would be, with a bit of help . . . ' Kathleen looked Rita over with a critical eye which made Rita squirm, and nodded. 'Yes, she certainly has potential. Um, look, tell you what, Rita. I'm going on from here to Mum's flat. I'm staying for a couple of days, see how she is, you know. I'll come and pick you up tomorrow and we'll have a day on the town, just you and me. Give us a chance to get to know each other, eh? Catch up on all the lost time. And I'll take you to a hairdresser – cut and perm, my treat. And some new clothes. I haven't been on a real shopping spree for ages. We'll get ourselves a couple of new outfits, and have lunch somewhere. What do you say?'

Rita said nothing. Kathleen was talking as if they

were a couple of buddies who had lost touch for a time. She was going to make up for abandoning her child by buying things for her. Then, no doubt, she would hop back on a train to Scotland and never be seen again. She was married, perhaps she had children who were Rita's half-brothers and sisters. The funny thing was, Rita didn't really want to know. This woman was a complete and embarrassing stranger, and Rita just wanted her to go away.

'Well, Rita?' Kathleen's smile wavered. 'Shall we do it?'

Pete answered for her. 'Rita would have to miss school, and I'm not sure that would be wise. Look, here's our telephone number.' He took a pencil and a small piece of paper from his pocket and scribbled hurriedly on it. 'Why don't you give us a call later tonight, and we'll sort something out then? I'm sorry, but I really will have to take Rita home now. I promised I'd be back soon, you see. Ready, Rita?'

Rita nodded. 'I'll just say goodbye to Gran.' She went into the ward, but Gran was fast asleep. When Rita came back outside, it was clear that Pete and Kathleen had not spoken to each other. They were both wearing vague smiles and looking in opposite directions.

'Goodbye,' said Rita and walked straight past Kathleen without looking at her.

''Bye Rita. Goodbye, Mr Brown. I'll see you tomorrow then.' Kathleen's voice had a forced brightness. Rita heard the heels clicking across the corridor as Kathleen went back into the ward. She put her hand in her pocket and fingered the front door key to the flat that she had picked up with her things. She had to get to the flat before Kathleen

105

returned there. The thought of this woman touching Rita's things, poking about in her room and sleeping in her bed, was intolerable.

'Pete, are we really in a hurry?' she asked.

He grinned. 'No. I'm on a course tomorrow, so my shift is covered tonight. You just looked as if you'd had enough.'

'Thanks.' Rita felt her eyes begin to water. 'Isn't she horrible? She's my mum and she's . . . awful!' She couldn't hold back any longer. She turned her face into Pete's shoulder and sobbed, for once oblivious to the people walking by and to the fact that she was making an exhibition of herself. Pete hugged her and said nothing while she cried and cried. When she was a little calmer, he said, 'Look, Rita. She's a bit spoilt, a bit selfish, maybe. But I don't think she means to be hurtful. She's simply not able to see life from anyone's point of view but her own. Frankly, if she were my mum, I might want to dispose of her. But you're lucky, Rita. She's *not* your mum. Not in any way that counts. Your gran took over that job, and she did it well.'

Rita scrubbed her eyes with the handkerchief he offered her. 'You don't like Kathleen much, do you?' she said, and they both laughed.

When they reached the car, Pete said, 'Rita, why did you ask if we were in a hurry? Is there something you want to do?'

Rita hesitated. 'It's all right. I don't want to be a trouble . . . '

'Come on,' he said. 'Out with it!'

'I just wanted to go to the flat. I left something behind – a few things, actually.'

'I see. Have you got a key?'

Rita showed him her door key.

'Right. Fair enough – we'll go home via the flat. We'll have to be quick, mind, or Kathleen will be there.'

Pete was wonderful. He understood.

'Thanks,' muttered Rita awkwardly.

Back at the flat, with Pete waiting in the car, Rita feverishly gathered things into big black sacks. She emptied her cupboard and drawer, and gathered up everything that was hers from the flat, every personal memento. She even took the ornaments that she had bought as presents for Gran, and the photograph albums that held a record of their life together. She couldn't bear the thought that Kathleen would learn things about her, touch things that belonged to her, even be able to hold pictures of her.

In the kitchen was Gran's 'treasures' drawer, full to the brim of memories: little drawings that Rita had done at school when she was tiny, school reports, early attempts at pottery, and mother's day cards with 'Mother' crossed out and 'Gran' written in a clumsy young hand. Rita emptied the drawer into another sack. From the top of the wardrobe she took the clothes she had outgrown last summer, which Gran was intending to pass on to a neighbour, and she also took her winter coat, hat and gloves, and her wellington boots. The flat was small, and she and Gran had never had much. In fifteen minutes the work was done, and Rita looked round her with satisfaction. There was not the slightest trace of Rita Dennison in this flat. She had even stripped her bed, and put the sheets and pillowcases into one of the sacks, tossing the blankets into the wardrobe and shutting the door. Nothing that Kathleen could touch would be anything to do with Rita now. It was tempting to take the food and the kettle, and to vandalize the place so that Kathleen would be very uncomfortable. But loyalty to Gran, who had brought her up to know better, stopped Rita from going this far.

Pete smiled at the four bulging black sacks Rita heaved into the street. 'Did you leave the kitchen sink behind, Rita?'

She smiled, feeling slightly high. 'Yes, but only just. I couldn't get it off the wall!'

Rita felt glorious. She had deprived her mother of any knowledge of Rita, just the way Rita had been deprived of any knowledge about Kathleen. She could poke and pry as much as she wanted. Rita had gone. It was like emerging triumphant from a great battle. She laughed and chatted away to Pete, daringly turning the music up on the radio without asking and commenting on everything she saw in a loud voice which sounded a bit strange even to her ears.

'Calm down, love,' said Pete gently as they got out of the car. He patted her on the shoulder, and Rita giggled helplessly at the thought of Kathleen rushing round the flat trying to find things.

'What on earth is the matter?' asked Annie as soon as she saw Rita.

'Kathleen turned up at the hospital,' said Pete.

'Oh Rita!' Annie held out her arms, and Rita found herself enfolded in yet another hug. The laughter turned into huge, gulping sobs that Rita thought would choke her, and Charlie started to cry too.

'Weeta not cwy!' he wailed.

'It's all right, Charlie. Come on, let's go and see what the others are watching on the telly, eh? Come on. It's all right.' Pete picked Charlie up and carried him from the room.

Annie still hung on to Rita, holding her tight while the sobs kept coming like a tide, until finally Rita stopped, exhausted.

'I bet that feels better,' she grinned and Rita, mopping her face with Pete's damp handkerchief, had to agree. She felt very, very tired but she also felt much calmer, as though she had regained control.

'You've had a rotten day, haven't you?' said Annie sympathetically. 'Never mind. It will pass, like all the other rotten days.'

'She's coming tomorrow,' said Rita.

'Who, Kathleen? Here? What for?'

'She's going to have my hair done and buy me new clothes.'

'Is she indeed?' Annie snorted. 'The cheek of it! What are you then, a Barbie doll?'

Rita smiled. 'Nothing so flash. I'm the raggedy-ann from the jumble sale.'

'Stop that!' said Annie. 'Stop doing that to yourself. It's time to stand up for who you really are, Rita Dennison. Not your gran's little mouthpiece, doing and saying all the right things. Not Kathleen's little dolly. Just you. Rita. All right?'

Rita nodded. Annie hugged her again.

'I think you're great,' said Annie. 'You have put up with so much, and you've coped so well. I couldn't have done it, I can tell you.'

Now was the time to tell her. Rita had not coped.

She had skived school, she had turned into a thief, she was going a bit mad. She had to open her mouth and force out the words. Now was the time.

'I think I'll go to bed,' she said. 'I'm really tired.'

'I should think you are,' said Annie. 'Off you go – do you want me to bring you a drink?'

Rita shook her head. She hadn't said it, and knew she wouldn't. Not today. 'Goodnight.'

10

'Your mother phoned last night.' Jody announced the news almost as soon as Rita opened her eyes. 'You were asleep – you need a lot of sleep, don't you?'

'Not usually,' said Rita defensively. Why did everything Jody say make her feel inadequate somehow? 'It's just with so much going on, I seem to get tired out.'

'Mmm. Well, you've got the day off school today. Your mum's picking you up at nine for a day out in town. Lucky you.' Jody picked up her school bag and swung out of the room.

Rita wished Jody could take her place. Jody would be a much more suitable daughter for Kathleen. She would love to be treated to new clothes and a haircut, and would not let Kathleen down in public as Rita knew she must. She had nothing smart to wear at all. The closest she could come to 'best' was a washed-out looking turquoise dress that she had chosen from Gran's catalogue for her birthday. She liked it, and it was comfortable, but Rita just knew, by instinct, that Kathleen would think it plain and dowdy. She pulled it out from the wardrobe and laid it on the bed. Next to it she put her jeans and best jumper. The jumper was nice, but the jeans were wearing through at both knees, and the only other pair she had were in need of a wash. She thought about the track suit she had brought home from her trip to the flat, but it was crumpled and a bit short in the arms. Perhaps she'd be better off wearing her school clothes.

As Rita stood, unable to decide, Jody came back. 'What's up, Rita?'

'Nothing. It's just . . . I don't know what to wear.'

Jody looked in silence at the clothes on the bed. Rita flushed.

'I don't usually care much about clothes,' she said. 'It's just . . . ' she didn't know how to explain.

'What's your mum like?' said Jody.

'Like a magazine picture,' said Rita miserably.

'Ah. Look, why don't you borrow something of mine?'

Rita felt she would rather die. Things were bad enough without being made into a charity case by the likes of Jody. 'No thanks.'

'Suit yourself. I was only trying to help.' Incredibly, Jody sounded a bit hurt.

'I'm sorry,' said Rita. 'I didn't mean it like that. But you're a bit bigger than me, and I'd be better off scruffy than swamped.'

'I've got some stuff from last year,' said Jody. She opened one of her drawers and pulled out two skirts, a jumper and a simple T-shirt dress. 'I think the black skirt and red jumper would look good,' she said. 'The jumper looked awful on me, because of my hair.' She looked appraisingly at Rita. 'You've got lovely colouring.'

112

The compliment took Rita by surprise. She didn't know what to say.

'Take what you want,' said Jody. 'You can keep it all, if you like. It's no use to me.' It was the same carelessness with which she had given Rita a hairbrush. Rita realized that Jody didn't see it as charity at all; she was simply a generous person, used to sharing.

'Thanks, Jody,' said Rita. 'By the way, I'm sorry if I've been . . . well, touchy since I've been here.'

'Touchy doesn't come close,' grinned Jody. 'Prickly pear, more like. Doesn't matter. I get used to all sorts. You're not as bad as some.'

Rita winced. Jody may be generous but she was not blessed with tact and diplomacy. She simply stated the facts as she saw them.

'Have a nice time with your mum,' said Jody. 'I've got to go. 'Bye.'

''Bye.' Rita looked at her watch. Half past eight. She had better get a move on. She showered, washed her hair and rather guiltily borrowed Jody's hairdryer. Rita's hair was quite glossy when it was clean and newly-brushed, but she knew it would look like a haystack before long, so she scraped it back into a pony tail. She put on the skirt and jumper Jody had suggested. The skirt was a bit creased, but there was no time to iron it and anyway she felt a bit shy about asking. Looking at herself in the mirror Rita saw an ordinary teenager; not glamorous, but not small and insignificant either. She smiled shyly at her reflection in the mirror, and went downstairs.

The older children and Pete had all gone, and Annie was feeding Adam while Charlie sucked on a banana, squidging the half-eaten remains in his hands and mumbling to himself between mouthfuls. He gave Rita a happy smile. 'Weeta! Weeta!'

Rita smiled back, and patted Charlie on the head. 'Morning, sunshine.'

'You look lovely, Rita,' said Annie. 'I never realized there was such a pretty face under all that hair!'

Rita blushed. 'Thanks. It's Jody's stuff – she said I could borrow it. Is that all right?'

'Of course. I've put some toast in for you – should be popping up any moment.'

Rita's stomach was churning far too much to accept food, but she mechanically chewed her way through a piece of toast and jam. The dining room clock swept towards nine. The dreaded hour approached and passed. At five past nine, Rita said, 'Perhaps she isn't coming. I'd better get my school uniform on.'

'She's only a few minutes late,' said Annie. 'Give her until half-past.'

Rita cleared the table and started the washing-up. Every inch of her was tense, waiting for the doorbell or phone to ring. She hoped for the phone: a call to say Kathleen had changed her mind. But just after twenty past nine the doorbell rang through the house. Gnasher, instantly alert, lumbered to his feet and took up his position at the front door.

'Will you get that, Rita?' called Annie from upstairs.

'Tum in, tum in!' cried Charlie.

With a pounding heart, Rita gripped Gnasher by the collar, heaved him away from the door and opened it. Sure enough, it was Kathleen, in another immaculate suit.

'Hello. Come in. Um, Annie will be down in a minute – I think she's changing the baby.'

Rita stood awkwardly in the hallway. Gnasher sniffed cautiously at Kathleen, and buried his huge snout against her skirt. When Rita pulled him away, there were hairs and a smear of saliva on the fabric. With an air of disgust, Kathleen pulled a tissue from her handbag.

'What a creature,' she said. 'Can you get rid of him, Rita? This suit costs a fortune in dry cleaning as it is.'

With difficulty, Rita shoved Gnasher into the kitchen and shut the door. He barked twice in protest, and then they heard him thump down onto the floor.

'He's, um, a bit messy but he's lovely really. You look very nice,' said Rita politely.

'Ta. You look better today yourself – skirt's a bit creased. Won't they let you use the iron here?'

Rita did not have a chance to answer. Annie was coming down the stairs. She must have heard the question.

'Hello.' Annie extended a hand with a charming smile. 'I'm Annie Brown. You must be Kathleen.'

'Yes. Hello.' Kathleen smiled a brief, tense smile.

Charlie, who was following Annie, squealed with delight when he saw a new visitor. 'Tum in, tum in!' There was still breakfast crusted round his mouth. Kathleen did not look impressed.

'I don't want to rush you,' she said to Rita, 'but there's a bus just after half-past.'

'I'm ready,' said Rita.

115

'Good. I'll bring her back about tea-time, will that be all right with you Mrs Brown? I thought we could have a spot of lunch out.'

'That's fine,' said Annie. There was an awkward pause while everyone tried to think of something to say. Thankfully, Gnasher barked again.

'We'd better get going,' said Kathleen, 'so you can let that dog out again. Goodbye.'

Outside the house, the awkward silence seemed to settle on them. They were at the bus stop before Kathleen spoke. Rita wondered if she, too, had been racking her brains for a topic of conversation.

'So, how are you off for clothes?' asked Kathleen.

Rita shrugged, embarrassed. 'I do OK.'

'Where'd you get those?'

'They're Jody's – Annie's daughter,' explained Rita. She squirmed inside; the other people at the bus stop could hear them.

'Thought so. They look too expensive for your gran; she'd never buy anything quality. She never understood that better-made clothes were cheaper in the long run; it was one of the things we used to argue about. She was an old skinflint, my mum.'

'Perhaps she just didn't have the money,' said Rita, stung.

'Yes, well.' Kathleen lit up a cigarette. 'I work as a buyer for a big department store now – the biggest chain of shops in Scotland. Women's fashion. I got there in spite of the old biddy doing her best to bring me up with no sense of style at all. Don't you worry, Rita. I've got an eye for what suits a person, and I'll kit you out so you won't know yourself.'

116

'Just a new pair of jeans would be nice,' said Rita cautiously.

Kathleen laughed, drawing on her cigarette and narrowing her eyes as she looked at Rita through the smokey haze. 'Oh, I think we can do better than that, Rita.'

The shopping trip that followed remained in Rita's mind as a whirlwind mixture of excitement and humiliation. They moved from shop to shop; Kathleen seemed determined to see everything. She was so elegant, so assured. Shop assistants seemed eager to help her, and she chatted about style and cut with them while Rita obediently tried on whatever she was offered. Emerging from the changing room, she would be ordered to twirl round while Kathleen, and usually one of the assistants, assessed her with a critical eye. They didn't seem to need Rita's opinion. 'That colour's lovely on her' or 'She's a bit too narrow across the shoulders to carry that off' or 'Now that's better than the last one' filled the air around her, but only once did Kathleen ask, 'Do you like that one, Rita?' It was a fitted suit, which made Rita feel and look much older. The skirt was straight and a bit tight, and the jacket felt much too short, nipped in at the waist and then finishing in a little frill. She didn't like it, but couldn't say so.

'It's all right,' she said, longing for her old jeans.

'Mmm. I'm not sure, myself. Oh well, let's take it. It'll do for going out somewhere special – don't wear it for a boyfriend, mind!' Kathleen laughed with the assistant and Rita blushed.

By lunchtime Rita was the reluctant and awkward owner of two new dresses, a pair of trousers and a matching waistcoat, a sweatshirt that Kathleen had spotted on a 'reduced' rack and had insisted was too good a bargain to miss, and the suit. She felt like a small child being kitted out.. Her opinion had been sought on none of it. At first, she was overwhelmed with Kathleen's enthusiasm and sense of purpose, and allowed herself to be swept along, even enjoying the experience of being fussed over and spoiled for once. But by the time they were sitting at a cramped little table in an overpriced but elegant restaurant – Kathleen's choice again, since Rita's suggestion of a nearby McDonald's had been met with laughter – a small cold flame of anger had begun to burn.

'I really enjoyed that,' said Kathleen. 'Making up for lost time, I suppose. I've missed out on having a daughter to share shopping trips with. Ken – my husband – and I don't have children, in case you're interested. Looks like you'll be the last of the line, Rita.'

Rita wasn't interested, not really. She just wanted Kathleen to leave. 'It was good of you to spend so much money on me,' she said politely. In her heart she added, 'Even though it was all wasted. I wouldn't be seen dead in what you've chosen for me.'

'No, I had a good time. And you are my daughter, for heaven's sake.' Kathleen saw Rita's face darken, and lit a cigarette. 'I should have kept in touch, Rita. I can see that now. But it wasn't easy. When you're older, you'll understand better.'

Rita said nothing. Kathleen's cigarette smoke hung over her half-eaten salad. Rita coughed, and Kathleen, with a look of annoyance, stubbed the cigarette out and called the waitress to order coffee. She carried on with a kind of determined brightness; Rita could see she was getting angry, but her tone was light and cheerful.

'Hairdresser next, eh? You'd look so pretty with a decent haircut – and a perm. Yes, a crown of dark curls around your face, lovely. What do you say?'

'Whatever you want,' said Rita.

'It's your hair, Rita, not mine.'

'I'm so glad you noticed,' Rita wanted to say, but she didn't. She simply nodded.

'Well,' said Kathleen. She looked intently at Rita, willing her to say something. Rita looked out of the window at the busy stream of shoppers. 'Let's go,' said Kathleen.

Kathleen's first choice of hairdresser was fully booked all afternoon and could do nothing until the following day. The next one had two stylists off sick, and could manage a cut and blow dry but not a perm. Kathleen had set her mind on a perm for her daughter, but did not want to 'traipse around looking for a hairdresser that's not the best anyway' as she put it. So they went back to the first one and Kathleen made an appointment for the following day.

'I can't miss school again,' said Rita. 'It'll have to be after school.' She willed herself to add that she didn't want a haircut anyway. But she felt so cross and mixed-up by now that she thought if she said any more she would end up shouting, crying maybe, and telling Kathleen exactly what she thought of her. She didn't want to do that. Part of Rita actually wanted to get to know Kathleen, and to have a mother at last. Kathleen made her angry, but perhaps she was better than nothing. Maybe when they knew each other better . . . Rita didn't want to risk throwing it away.

'I was supposed to be meeting a friend tomorrow,' said Kathleen. 'Oh well, I suppose I can phone and try and arrange to meet her later. All right, half-past four, please.' The appointment was confirmed, and Rita's chance to object had passed.

Kathleen proposed that they spend the afternoon walking by the river which stretched through the centre of town, perhaps taking a trip on one of the boats which offered pleasure cruises. But Rita, conscious that this would leave lots of opportunities to talk, asked if they could go to the cinema instead. Kathleen took this as a sign that Rita was warming to her at last, and was very cheerful and chatty as they walked to the cinema. She told Rita about her life back in Scotland, and about Ken, who was a good man but had a bit of an eye for the ladies.

'He hasn't been unfaithful, though,' said Kathleen. 'I expect he knows he'd be shown the door. I may have made a mistake a long time ago, but since I've married Ken I've been a strictly a one-man woman.'

Rita was embarrassed. Kathleen should not be telling her all this. She was also angry. She, Rita, was supposedly the 'mistake' Kathleen had made. 'Does your husband know about me?' she asked.

Kathleen blushed slightly. 'Of course.'

'Didn't he want to come with you?' asked Rita. 'If I was in his place, I'd want to see my wife's child. I'd be curious to see what she looked like.'

Kathleen fished around in her bag for her cigarettes. They had to stop while she lit one. Rita saw

120

her hand shake slightly. 'He's interested, of course he is. I said I'd tell him all about you when I got back.'

'You're lying,' said Rita suddenly. 'He doesn't know, does he? I bet he thinks you're just here visiting friends or something.'

'All right, so he doesn't know. He knows about Mum, but not about you. How could I tell him I had a kid, when he's so broken up about us never being able to have any? It would cut him, Rita. You don't know him. P'raps one day. . . . '

'Don't bother telling him on my account,' said Rita. 'I couldn't care less if he knows or not.'

'You are such a sour little puss!' said Kathleen angrily. 'I've tried to take an interest, I've spent a fortune on you, I've tried to explain what's gone on in the past, but you just won't give me a chance, will you? What do you want from me, Rita? Eh? Can't you see I'm doing my best? I just can't tell what you *want* from me.' Kathleen's voice rose into a shrill, childlike whine, and to Rita's horror she started to cry. Little pools of watery fluid collected at the bottom of her eyes, flecked with mascara. Carefully, Kathleen dabbed at her eyes with a small handkerchief. It came away from her face smudged with black.

'Sorry,' said Rita. The anger melted away, but she didn't feel sorry for her mother, just awkward. People were looking at them. 'Don't cry.'

'It's OK,' said Kathleen with a bad attempt at a smile. 'It's all the travelling and worrying about Mum, and meeting you and – all sorts of things. I'm fine, really I am. Now, what film do you want to see?'

Rita didn't want to see a film. She was desperate for this outing to end. 'Can we skip the film? Thing is, I've got so much homework, I wouldn't mind the chance to catch up since I'm off school anyway,' she lied. 'And we'll see each other tomorrow, won't we?'

'Yes, all right. Come on then, I'll see you home.'

'No need,' said Rita hastily. 'I can get the bus on my own. Why don't you go and see Gran? She'd love to see you, and you could tell her Pete's bringing me in tonight. Yeah?'

Kathleen nodded. Rita could tell she was relieved. Kathleen had not enjoyed this meeting any more than Rita had. At once Rita felt rejected, and the cold flame started burning in her stomach again.

'If that's the way you want it, Rita, that's fine by me. I won't see you tonight – I've promised to go round to see someone. But I'll phone in the morning and arrange to meet for the hairdresser's, eh? We'll have a good laugh together, you and me. You'll look so grown up with your new hairstyle, maybe I'll take you down the pub and see if they'll let you in. We used to do that all the time when I was your age.'

Rita squirmed. Tomorrow would be just as bad as today, but at least it was tomorrow. 'Yeah, sounds great. Look, I'd better go. 'Bye.'

She took the bags Kathleen offered her and set off for the bus stop. When she looked back, Kathleen was still in the same spot, watching her. She waved at Rita, and then turned and walked quickly away in the opposite direction. Rita breathed a sigh of relief.

It was only three o'clock when Rita reached the

Browns'. Annie and her mother were in the living room, where Rosie was amusing the babies while Annie got on with the ironing. Gnasher greeted her with enthusiasm, but Rosie and Annie looked concerned.

'You're back early,' said Annie. There was a question in her eyes.

'We finished shopping,' said Rita. 'We're going out again, to the hairdresser's, tomorrow.'

'Did you have a good time?' asked Rosie.

'It was all right,' said Rita.

Annie and Rosie exchanged glances. 'You certainly seem to have done well out of it,' said Rosie, nodding at the bags. 'What have you got there?'

Without enthusiasm, Rita opened the bags and let Rosie peep inside.

'She's certainly splashed out on you, hasn't she?' said Rosie. There was a tone of disapproval that Rita understood. Rosie had no time for a woman who abandoned her own child and then tried to buy her affection with a few clothes. It was the sort of reaction Gran would have.

'Why don't you try them on, Rita, and give us a fashion show. We'd love to see a twirl, wouldn't we Charlie?'

'Tirl, Weeta,' said Charlie, laughing. He had no idea what it meant, but it sounded like a good game.

Rita gathered her bags and went upstairs. She sat at Jody's dressing table, littered with make-up, nail polish, hairbands and used cotton buds. She studied her face in the mirror, searching for a likeness to Kathleen. Only the colour and straightness of hair seemed to match. Except of course that Kathleen's hair was immaculate, whereas Rita's

123

was always a mess. Slowly she pulled out the band holding it back, and it fell round her face. Kathleen was going to change all that. Tomorrow the miracle of the transformation of the ugly duckling would be completed. A simple perm and a change of clothes would do the trick.

Kathleen had not asked Rita's opinion, just as Gran had never asked. Rita was simply told what to do, and she did it. That was the way of things. That was the way it had always been. Until now.

Slowly, Rita picked up Jody's nail scissors. The first few snips came just below her ears, but as the dark snakes of hair started to fall away from her head, Rita became more and more fevered. In the end, she was cutting her hair as close to the scalp as she could manoeuvre the little scissors. When she had finished, and there was almost no hair left to cut, Rita carefully gathered it all up and stuffed it into one of her school socks.

'Try changing me now, Kathleen,' she said aloud. Then she put the hair in the drawer with the things she had stolen, and started to undress.

11

Jody was the first to see her. Rita heard her come in with Jason, greeting Gnasher and complaining about all the homework she had. There was a murmur of conversation and then Rita heard her climbing the stairs. She sat on the bed, in the suit her mother had chosen for her, staring straight ahead so that her eyes did not catch a mirror.

'Mum and Gran want to know when you're coming. . . . Oh my God – what have you *done?*' Jody's green eyes glowed with horror. She looked at Rita as if she were stark raving mad. But Rita felt perfectly calm and in control. She was not quite a part of the world; it was like being in someone else's dream, where you could watch what was happening and not feel frightened by it. For too long, she had let other people decide who she was, what she thought and what she could do. Now she had simply reclaimed her own life. Rita didn't care what anyone else thought, in fact, she rather enjoyed the idea of shocking those who thought she was a quiet little mouse with no ideas of her own: like Jody, and Kathleen. She felt free, and powerful, a feeling which was only strengthened by Jody's shocked disbelief.

'I fancied it short,' Rita said, fingering her hair. She smiled at Jody.

Jody took a step backwards. '*Mum!*' she called suddenly, her voice rising almost to a scream. '*Mum, come here!*'

Rita stood, waiting, as the confusion of footsteps headed for Jody's room. Annie arrived first, with Rosie at her shoulder almost immediately afterwards. She had Charlie balanced on her hip. Annie's hand flew to her mouth. She looked back at Rosie. 'Rita. . . . ' she said. Charlie was silent for a moment as he stared solemnly at Rita, not recognizing her. Then he laughed, a great belly laugh. 'Weeta!' he squealed. 'Weeta hair all gone!'

Jason pushed his way past Annie and Rosie and came right up to Rita with wide eyes. 'Where's all your hair gone?' he asked. His face quivered. He didn't know whether to cry or laugh. Was this a joke, or had something terrible happened to Rita? Perhaps there were people here, as well as at his old house, who liked to hurt children. Perhaps he was not as safe as he had thought. 'Who did it?' he asked anxiously.

Rita didn't understand why he should look so afraid, but she touched his cheek reassuringly. 'I did it. I thought I'd save Kathleen the trouble and expense. She'll have a bit of a job having this permed, won't she?' Rita laughed, and fingered the sticks of hair which still clung to her scalp.

'You're mad!' said Jody. She turned to her mother. 'She's completely out of her tree!'

'Jody, shut up! Go and lay the table for tea.' Annie's angry tone subdued Jody only slightly. She started to speak again. 'I said *go!*' thundered Annie, and Jody left, with one last withering look at her room-mate.

'You won't hurt me, will you Rita?' said Jason. He was ninety-nine per cent sure, but still had to ask.

'Of course not. You're my best friend,' said Rita. Jason hugged her around her waist, and she laid a hand on his head.

'What's all the fuss about?' asked Mark. 'Jody looks as though she's seen a ghost!' His face fell as he peered over Annie's shoulder. 'Wow! Is this a new fashion?'

'Not now, Mark,' said Rosie quietly. 'Go and help Jody with the tea, will you? And take Jason.'

'Oh, like that is it? Right.' Mark disappeared, holding Jason's hand, with another quizzical look at Rita. As they went back downstairs, Rita could hear the boys chuckling. About her, probably. She must look strange.

'Rita, why did you do it?' asked Annie. She put Charlie down and he headed for Jody's make-up unchecked as Annie and Rosie came over to Rita. Annie touched the shorn ends. 'Oh, Rita. This will take forever to grow again. What have you done?'

'You told me to take control,' said Rita. 'Well, I did. Kathleen's determined to change me, and I'm just getting in first. After all, it's my hair, isn't it? I should be the one to choose what happens to it, not her. I never liked it long anyway. It was always messy. This'll be much easier.' Self-consciously, she fingered her scalp again. There did seem to be some very thin patches.

Rita turned around to face the mirror and got the shock of her life. She had been in such a state,

127

she had not known what she was doing. Towards the end she had not been looking in the mirror at all. In her mind it was the kind of salon haircut some of her friends had: short, a bit spiky, quite attractive when you got used to it. Now, facing the nightmare reflection in front of her, Rita realized the enormity of what she had done to herself.

In some places, Rita had cut her hair so close to the scalp that she was almost bald. In others, long wisps of hair sprouted from short stubby patches that stood on end. No wonder Jody had called her mad. She looked like someone from another planet. All the composure she thought she had disappeared in a flash. Her wild eyes were exposed and she could not hide her panic behind that handy veil of hair any more.

'It's a mess, isn't it?' she said weakly. She was past crying.

'It's a mess,' confirmed Annie. 'Now are you going to tell us what this is all about? It's a hell of a way to get attention, Rita.'

Was that it? Was that why she had done it? Rita had thought it was just a way of stopping Kathleen having control of her life. But perhaps Annie was right. Perhaps she was trying to get them to look at her more closely. Can't you see? she said inside her head. Can't you see that I'm only pretending to be all right? My life's a mess and I need help. This is not the half of it. Can't you see what else I've done?

'I don't know,' she said slowly. 'I was upset – about Kathleen, and her wanting to buy me things and have my hair done. We went to all these shops, loads of them, and she just . . . it was like being a doll, you know? She dressed me the way she wanted me. She never asked what I thought. It didn't matter to her. And I got angry. It felt like she had no right, you know? No right to make decisions like that. And the only way to stop her was this.' She pointed to her hair.

'It wasn't the only way, Rita,' said Annie. Rita could tell she was trying not to sound exasperated. 'When I said you should take control I meant stand up for yourself, not this . . . mutilation. Why couldn't you just have told her you didn't want a different hairstyle?'

Rita was silent.

'Annie's right,' said Rosie. 'All you had to do was say, "Look, I'm fine as I am, thank you". Why couldn't you do that?'

'Because I'm *not* fine. I didn't like my hair the way it was. I didn't like *anything* the way it was. Kathleen was right – and Jody, when she first saw me. I'm ugly and stupid, and now I've just made things even worse. And on top of all that, I. . . . '

She couldn't hold back the tears. Rosie made a move towards her, but Annie caught her arm. 'What?' she said calmly. 'Come on, spit it out. What else have you been up to, Miss Rita Dennison? Eh? What else is going on in that poor shorn head of yours?'

Rita didn't know where to start. She wanted to tell Annie about skiving off school, and stealing things, and it no longer mattered what Annie and Pete thought of her. How could their opinion get any lower anyway? She just couldn't find the words.

'Will it help if I tell you that I phoned school today, to tell them you wouldn't be in?' asked

Annie. She nodded as she met Rita's eyes. 'Yes. They told me. You haven't been going to school.'

'What?' Rosie gasped. 'You've never been playing truant, Rita?'

Rita hung her head.

'Yes, Mum, Rita's been skiving school. Where have you been instead, Rita? What have you been doing? You may as well tell us.'

She was right. Rita had nothing to lose now. 'I've never done it before,' whispered Rita. 'I can't stop myself doing things, really stupid things, since Gran got ill. I just can't.'

'What things? What have you done?' asked Annie.

'Annie, I don't think. . . . ' said Rosie nervously. Annie was still holding her arm. She let go, and smiled reassuringly at her mother. 'It's all right, Mum. I think there's more. I think Rita wants to tell us. It's time to get this all straightened out. Now, I'm going to get a trip to the park organized for Jason and Charlie, and then I'm going to come back up here and we're going to sort all of this out. All of it, Rita. OK?'

Rita nodded. Annie picked up Charlie. Neither of them commented on the bright smears of lipstick and eyeshadow across his mouth and cheek. Rita didn't squash a grim satisfaction in knowing that Jody would hit the roof when she saw it. Annie went downstairs, and Rosie sat on Jody's bed. She didn't know what to do, or say, except, 'Oh Rita, lovey.'

Rita crouched down by the bed and pulled out all the stolen things. They piled up and spilled over on the floor, everything she had stolen. She picked up the items, one by one, and arranged them neatly on the carpet. There were more than she thought. Then she laid out her hair, a tangled mess of darkness on the pale carpet. This was the last of the old Rita, the one who hid herself and did as she was told.

'What on earth is all this, Rita?' asked Rosie. When Rita didn't answer, she sighed and came to sit next to Rita on the floor. She put her arm around her, and Rita leaned against the comfortable softness. Neither of them spoke.

Jody's voice rose predictably in anger when she saw Charlie, and Rita's own name was audible several times in the murmur of Jody's lament to her mother. There was a scraping of chairs, a crashing of plates and cups: Rita pictured them all leaving in her mind. Jason would be holding Mark's hand and Jody would be pushing Charlie in the buggy; perhaps they were taking Adam too, although Rita thought he was asleep. They would have to dodge past Gnasher, who got very excited whenever he saw the children putting their coats on. The front door slammed, hard – Jody. Rita pictured her with eyes blazing, head high, storming down the street and telling Mark about the indignities that she had to suffer in this family. Charlie's face would still be covered in make-up; there would have been no time to wash it, unless Gnasher had obliged.

All this Rita pictured, and knew she would have to leave. 'You stupid little idiot,' she told herself. 'It's just typical of you to spoil it. You could have been happy here, Rita Dennison.' It was true. Rita didn't want to be disloyal to Gran, but she felt more a part of this family than she did of her own. If she hadn't been so stupid, they might have let her come and visit, even stay sometimes, after Gran got out of hospital. No chance now, the inner voice said viciously. Rita watched the closed bedroom door which would soon open to Annie for the 'sorting out'. There was more to sort out than Annie knew.

Rosie was rocking her, very gently, like she did with Charlie when he was tired, and she was stroking Rita's face. It felt lovely, and made her feel watery and ready to sleep. The telephone rang, and was answered. Rita couldn't hear anything for a while after that.

Rita pictured Gran, lying in bed and waiting for her granddaughter to visit. What would they tell her? How could Rita face her, looking like this? She was an old lady, easily shocked. The stroke had made Rita realize that Gran was not going to stay the same for ever, doing a hundred things at once. She was getting old, and Rita's children would probably never know her. Where's your mummy and daddy? they would ask Rita, and what would she say? Oh yes, I do have a mummy, but she doesn't much like me so she never comes to call? Would Rita pretend Kathleen didn't exist, the way Gran had pretended all those years? And what would it be like for Kathleen, to have her existence denied like that? Not that Rita cared, not really. She hated Kathleen, who had spoiled things for her here in the first proper family Rita had ever known.

The door opened. It was Annie, pushing against the door with her back and carrying a loaded tray. Rosie sprang up to help.

'Well,' said Annie softly. 'This is an adventure

132

and a half, isn't it? Never mind. It'll sort itself out in the end.'

She had not really taken in the significance of the array of things on the floor at first, but she caught Rosie's pointed look and followed her mother's eyes to the pile of goods on the floor. 'What are all these things, Rita? They're not yours, are they?'

Rita shook her head. Annie looked at her, waiting for more information. Then, getting nothing, she knelt to examine the pile of things more closely. 'But they're all brand new,' she said. 'And look at all the sizes . . . are you buying presents for people, Rita?'

Rita hung her head. She wished she could be struck dead by a sudden thunderbolt, but there was no escape. She said nothing.

Annie was clearly mystified. 'What on earth would anyone want with this . . . these are very expensive. Rita, where has all this stuff come from?'

Rita couldn't answer. She looked at the window, and wondered if it would be worth trying to jump out of it and run away. She would probably only break a leg.

'She's taken them, Annie,' said Rosie calmly. 'That must be what she was doing when she should have been in school. You've been out thieving, haven't you, Rita?'

Rita's face was burning. She nodded, briefly.

'Rita, why? Why on earth . . . oh, listen to me. I don't suppose you know any more than I do, do you? What a mess.' Annie sighed.

'I can't stop myself,' said Rita. 'I think I might be going mad. I can't help doing it . . . where will they send me, do you think?'

'No-one's sending you anywhere!' snorted Rosie. 'Listen, pet, you're obviously not yourself. That's not the same as mad, mind, not the same at all. There'll be no need for going away, I can tell you that.'

'What will they do?' asked Rita, her heart pounding.

'I don't know, lovey, I really don't,' said Rosie. She looked at Annie.

'If by "they" you mean social services, I'm not sure myself. We'll have to tell Wendy, and maybe she'll know what to do. I don't suppose you're the first to get into this sort of scrape.'

'I'm ever so sorry,' said Rita. It seemed hopelessly inadequate, but she couldn't think of anything else.

Rosie laughed, and put her arms around Rita again. 'That hairstyle beats all, it really does.'

Rita felt her lips move into a small smile. 'Do you think Kathleen will like it?'

'Funny you should mention Kathleen,' said Annie with a grim smile. 'That was her on the phone. She can't make it tomorrow after all. She's got to go back to Scotland in the morning – some crisis at work. She might be able to see you tonight before she leaves, but she doubts it. She asked me to say goodbye and good luck to you.'

So Rita had chopped her hair off for nothing. Kathleen could not even be bothered to say goodbye herself. That was that. Rita started to laugh, and then to cry, and then seemed to be doing both at once. There was nothing Rita wanted more than for Kathleen to be hundreds of miles away so that she could start to forget she had ever existed at all:

so why did she feel as though something had been suddenly torn from her?

'I can't take it,' she sobbed. 'I just want it to stop – all of it. I just want to fall asleep and never wake up.'

'I'll bet,' said Annie. 'It would be awfully handy to have a wand waved over you right now, wouldn't it? You could fall asleep for a hundred years and wake up to a handsome prince. But I'm afraid this is the real world, pet, and what you've done has got to be faced up to. Look, I've called Wendy, and she'll be here any minute. Pete will be in soon, too. Then there'll be more things to explain,' she nodded at the pile of stolen goods on the floor, 'and decisions to be made.'

Rita nodded. Decisions. What to tell Gran – and the police. She supposed they would have to take her to the station to confess. Gran would die of shame. Maybe they would tell Kathleen, who would shrug her shoulders and thank her lucky stars she had left the kid, who was obviously a wrong 'un.

12

Wendy sat on Jody's bed, opposite Rita. She seemed to be at a loss for words. She looked from Rita's scraggy ends of hair to the display of things Rita had stolen from the shops and back to Rita, who sat with her head bowed.

'Oh, Rita!' was all Wendy could say.

Rita said nothing. What was there to say? She waited for Wendy to pronounce judgement, to tell her what to do.

'What are you going to do about all this, Rita?' asked Wendy.

Rita looked up in surprise. What did she mean, what was Rita going to do? It was surely her job to work out what to do and make sure Rita did it. The question left Rita confused.

'I don't know,' she said. 'What do you want me to do?'

Wendy smiled. 'Oh no you don't.'

'What do you mean?' asked Rita.

Wendy sighed. 'Look, Rita. You wouldn't be in this mess in the first place if you'd thought through what *you* wanted and then taken a stand for it. Ever since we met you've been waiting to be told what to do. You've never said how you felt, never really made a decision. Now, I suppose I could work out a plan of action and you could obey my orders like a little puppet doll. But somewhere along the line you've got to get back on an even keel and get your life back together again. So why don't we start now?'

Rita squirmed inside. What Wendy was saying was that she, Rita, had been behaving like a real wimp these past few days. That hurt. It might be true, but it still stung to hear it said by some woman who didn't even know what Rita was really like.

'It's not easy, you know,' she said suddenly. 'I just feel so. . . . '

'Go on, Rita,' said Wendy gently. 'What do you feel about all this, exactly?'

'Lost,' said Rita briefly. It was like being cast adrift in a little boat, and told to head for the next harbour, when you had no idea where it was. So you paddled off, hoping that you would find somewhere before a storm swamped your little boat and drowned you in a raging ocean. That was how Rita felt about all this. But how could she tell Wendy? Rita's gran had brought her up to 'keep herself to herself', to 'keep private grief private' and to 'put on a brave face'. Gran would never admit weakness, or fear, and Rita could not do it either. Gran would understand without words and would know what to do. But Gran was too ill to be landed with Rita's problems, and Wendy was not prepared to help her.

'I know I've been really stupid,' Rita said at last. 'I don't know why I stole all those things, or why I cut my hair, not really. I've done wrong and I'm ready to be punished. Just tell me what to do, and

I'll do it. Whatever you say – just let's get it over with.'

Wendy shook her head. 'No. I'm not going to tell you what to do, Rita. I think you can work it out for yourself.'

Rita wanted to throw something at her. 'It's your job!' she said. 'What use is a social worker who doesn't know what to do? Annie said you'd have seen all this before. Am I the only one in the world who's been out nicking things?'

Again, Wendy shook her head. A small, hard smile played on her lips and was stilled. 'You're an intelligent young woman, Rita. I'm just waiting to hear your own ideas about how we can put this right before I offer an opinion. OK?'

Rita could see that they were at a stalemate. Wendy was not going to tell her what to do. It became clear that she was not going to leave, either, until Rita spoke. For a long time they sat in silence in the bedroom, with the bustle of the Brown family all around them in the house. Rita's nerve cracked first.

'All right,' she said savagely. 'I want to put it right. If you won't help me, at least tell me this. Do you have to go to the police?'

'Depends,' said Wendy. She was watching Rita carefully. Really, the woman was infuriating.

'Depends on what?'

'On what your alternative might be.'

There was another silence while Rita digested this. Then she said, 'The things will have to go back, won't they?'

Wendy said, 'What do you think?'

I think, said Rita silently, that I am going to have

to wring your neck in a minute. Aloud she said, 'I think they have to go back. I could send them through the post, with a note saying I'm sorry. Yes, that would work. I think I can remember where everything came from, and the labels will help. I could take them back in person, of course, only. . . . '

'Yes?' Wendy raised an eyebrow.

'Well, I haven't the guts for one thing. I mean, how can I stroll in with a pair of size eighteen underpants and say, "Sorry, these just jumped into my hand somehow. . . . " They would think I was nuts, wouldn't they?'

Wendy looked pointedly at Rita's new hairstyle, and nodded.

'OK, so I'll make up parcels with the stuff inside and send everything back anonymously.' Now that she had thought of it, it seemed such a simple solution that Rita couldn't understand why she hadn't done it before. 'Will that be all right?'

'I think so. You're not a hardened criminal, and I think you've learned a lesson from it, too. All in all, I think sending the things back would be acceptable. What else?'

Rita was startled. 'I didn't take anything else.'

Wendy smiled. 'I know. I was talking about the other things. Like school, like your mother, like the Browns. What are you going to do about them? And what are you going to tell your grandmother?'

Rita felt the ocean beginning to swell beneath her little boat. 'I don't know. It's too much.'

'No it isn't, Rita. Just think about one thing at a time. Don't let it drown you. Look at one thing, and decide what to do.'

Wendy made it sound easy; perhaps it was worth a try. Rita sighed. 'School. There'll be hell to pay. But they know about Gran, and my form teacher is a softy. If I put on the agony a bit, play the part of the poor little girl whose mind became temporarily deranged because of her problems at home, they'll probably let me off.' Rita grinned, and Wendy laughed.

'You're doing very well so far, Rita,' she said. 'What next?'

'Jody,' said Rita. 'While it would be good to let the school think I went a bit nutty, the exact opposite would be wise for Jody. I could take a test of sanity, or something. And wear a hat.' She fingered her hair. 'If the Browns let me stay, of course. Do you think they will? Or do I have to work that out for myself, too?'

'No. I'll talk to the Browns. But I'm pretty sure it'll be all right. It's likely only to be another week or two anyway. I've spoken to the hospital and your gran's doing well. It may be possible to get home help and a community nurse to come in and see her at home. The neighbours are willing to rally round, and you'll be able to do a lot for her. I'm not promising, mind, but it looks more hopeful than it did when your gran had the stroke.'

'So that's that. I'll get by Gran somehow. She's bound to notice my hair's gone, even if I wear a hat, but she doesn't have to know why I did it. I'll say I was trying to look like someone I saw on "Top of the Pops" and it went a bit wrong. She'll fall for that – she thinks "Top of the Pops" is a corrupting influence on young minds.'

'Good work,' said Wendy, and smiled encouragingly. 'There's only one loose end now, isn't there? What are you going to do about Kathleen?'

'Nothing,' said Rita. 'I don't need to do anything.'

'Don't you think you should talk to her, Rita, and let her know how you feel?'

Why not? Rita felt in no danger from Kathleen now, not over the telephone, and Kathleen was on her way back to Scotland. 'Definitely,' she said. 'I must definitely tell Kathleen that she has no right to try and run my life after dumping me when I was only a baby. And if she ever comes back here again, I'll tell her that to her face.'

'I'm glad you said that,' said Wendy. 'Kathleen called me at the office only five minutes before Annie did. She said she was going back to Scotland, but wanted to be kept informed about you and your gran.' Wendy paused. 'I told her I thought it would be a very bad idea to go back to Scotland without saying goodbye in person. So she's agreed to get the overnight train so that she can see you one more time.'

'What?' Rita's knees turned to water. 'Oh no. Look, I can't go and see her like this, can I? She already thinks I'm a right dipstick. Seeing me like this will just make her sure of it.'

'Wear a hat,' grinned Wendy.

'Ho, ho.'

Wendy stood up. 'I've got to go,' she said. 'I want to have a word with Annie and Pete before I go. But I've arranged to meet Kathleen at the hospital at seven. Pete will take you in when he goes to work. You'll have a chance to visit your gran, say goodbye to your mother and start afresh with the

Browns. Well done, Rita. You've got your act together quite wonderfully.'

Wendy left with a big, beaming smile over her shoulder at Rita. 'Good luck!' she said. Rita had a weird feeling that Wendy had steered her right through their conversation, even though Rita had been the one apparently making all the decisions.

No sooner had the door closed behind Wendy than it opened to reveal Jody, carrying a mug of tea and a plate of buttered toast. She offered it to Rita. Sensing that it was some kind of peace gesture, Rita took a slice. Jody's eyes did not leave Rita's hair.

'It'll take ages to grow,' said Jody finally. 'What are you going to do?'

'Wear a hat,' said Rita. She grabbed a towel from the end of her bed and wrapped it clumsily round her head. 'Or a turban.'

Jody laughed. 'You'll look like a nutter.'

'P'raps I am one.'

'Yes, perhaps you are. Ah well, I suppose it's better than being boring ordinary.'

Neither of them knew what to say next. Rita sensed that Jody wanted to talk, but didn't know how to begin. Rita realized that she had never really given Jody a chance, not since that first awful minute when Jody's eyes had swept over and dismissed the new foster child as if she were no more than a piece of furniture. Now Rita knew that Jody was not tactful, but she was not deliberately unkind either.

'Jody . . .'

'What?'

'Would you . . . I mean, if you've got time, could

you . . . help me get out of this mess?' Rita pointed to her head. 'Wendy has fixed it for me to see my mum one last time, and I've got to face Gran, too. I don't know how to disguise it.'

Jody delivered another of her long, sweeping looks, assessing the situation coolly. Then she smiled. 'It'll certainly be a challenge,' she said. 'But let's face it, nothing I could do would make it look worse, would it?'

'Don't spare me, Jody, just give it to me straight!' smiled Rita. For the first time she felt Jody's equal, which was curious because it was the first time she had asked for Jody's help.

Jody stood up. 'The first bit is easy – I'll phone Aunty Peg. She's a hairdresser.'

'No!' Rita was horrified. 'I can't go into a hairdresser's looking like this!'

'Precisely,' said Jody coolly. 'That's why it has to be Aunty Peg. I am her favourite niece, and if I ask her to come she'll be here, no worries. I'll have to tell her what state it's in, though, so she comes prepared. . . . '

'What will you tell her?'

Jody smiled. 'The truth. That we have a new kid who went a bit bananas – '

'Thanks a lot,' muttered Rita.

'Who went a bit bananas but is OK now and needs a bit of expert help,' finished Jody. 'It'll be all right. She's a bit weird herself, so she'll take to you, I expect.'

And so it was. Aunty Peg, who turned out to be Pete's younger sister, came round within an hour of Jody's call. Rita couldn't face being stared at over dinner, and Jody brought up a tray so that

Rita could eat in their room. By the time Peg arrived, Rita was feeling a bit like a prisoner. Peg laughed heartily and without inhibition at Rita's miserable face shrouded in black shaggy tufts of hair. 'Whoo!' she said. 'I don't think that style will catch on, ducks, do you?'

Rita shook her head. 'Can you do anything?' she asked.

Peg nodded and started to rummage in her bag. 'Oh yes,' she said. 'You've left your scalp intact, and for that we should be grateful. Now, sit up straight and leave it to me.'

Half an hour later, including a nerve-wracking spell where Peg seemed to be shaving Rita's head, it was all over, and Rita approached a mirror.

She now had almost no hair at all, but it was the same all over her head. She looked a bit like an American soldier. Rita held her head this way and that, trying to get used to it. Her eyes looked huge, and her cheekbones stood out, somehow. It was not Rita staring back at her, but a new being. She felt stronger, more powerful, even a bit daring.

'What do you think?' asked Peg.

'I think it's . . . I think I like it, you know?' said Rita.

'You've got a beautifully shaped head,' said Peg. 'No, honestly, I'm not just saying it. Beautifully balanced, it is. You look like a pop star – a bit weird, but wonderful. You need pierced ears, really, and big dangly earrings, and you'll look marvellous.'

'Yes, I see what you mean,' said Rita. 'I might just do that.'

She thanked Peg, and they went downstairs

together. The whole family was waiting in the living room. Everyone was anxious to see what Rita looked like, and how she felt. It was like being in a big, warm bath full of care and affection. After the initial moment of shocked silence, it was generally agreed that Peg had done a good job. Mark and Jody pronounced the new style 'brilliant' and Jody said she wished she had the guts to try it for herself. Charlie squealed with laughter and then insisted on stroking and restroking Rita's head. Jason joined in, and declared Rita's head to be just like a fluffy chicken. Even Annie seemed genuinely surprised at how good a job Peg had been able to do. Rita felt relaxed and almost happy, much more like the old Rita before Gran's stroke. But she still had to face Kathleen, and her gran. Rita hoped the new feeling would last.

13

Rita spent a lot of time getting ready to go to the hospital that night. She had a shower, washed her head and dusted herself all over with the sweet-smelling talcum powder that stood in a big tub in the bathroom. She pulled on her best jeans, the ones she felt most comfortable in without being too scruffy, and donned the sweatshirt Kathleen had bought her. Then she let Jody smooth some cream into her skin; it smelled of roses and honey, and Jody said it would make her skin feel soft. It did. Jody also spread a little bit of blusher on Rita's cheek bones, to accentuate them, and persuaded her to use a little bit of mascara and plain lip gloss. Rita had never been able to get the hang of make-up; she always scrubbed it off when she put it on with her friends, because she felt like a crude, cheap plastic doll. But Jody was experienced, and had a natural skill. She showed Rita how to choose subtle colours, and not to use too much. Rita looked at herself in the mirror with pride. She felt almost beautiful.

'You look so good!' breathed Jody, and the look of disbelief on her face was all the praise Rita could want. She still didn't feel completely at ease with this look; she missed the shield of hair very much, and felt exposed now that she couldn't hide behind it any more. But she liked it, and in time she would be more confident.

First she had to clear up the mess she had made with her life, though. Kathleen, Gran, and then the stolen things to be returned; after that (and facing the music for bunking off school) she could begin to get her life together again. She had been behaving like a wimp, but now she felt more like her old self. In fact, in the car on the way to hospital Rita realized that losing her hair made her feel like a bit of her old self had been returned with something added on. This thought made her laugh, and Pete asked if she was all right.

Pete drove Rita to the hospital almost in silence, sensing that she needed the time to think. What could she say to Kathleen? There were hundreds of things she wanted to say, or questions to ask, but none of them were very polite. Rita hoped she would never have to think about Kathleen again, still less see her, but deep down she also wanted them to part on friendly terms. On the other hand, she didn't want a cosy mummy-daughter reunion. Kathleen would never feel like a mother, and Rita didn't want to have to pretend. Working out what to say in words that would get the message across without hurting Kathleen too much was going to be pretty impossible.

Pete left Rita just outside the ward and went off to work. Wendy was waiting for Rita. She smiled nervously.

'You look very different,' she said. 'It's quite nice, Rita.'

'I like it,' said Rita defensively.

'Well that's the main thing, isn't it?' said Wendy vaguely. 'Your mum's here, Rita. The sister has given us a quiet room to meet in, so we can talk. OK?'

Rita nodded, and followed Wendy past the ward and down a long corridor. Her heart was pounding and something hot and nasty-tasting was flowing from her throat into her stomach – or perhaps it was the other way round, she couldn't tell. She felt scared, but couldn't identify what it was she was scared of. Nothing was going to happen to her here, in this quiet hospital with Wendy right beside her. Yet she still felt scared to death, and could hardly choke out a greeting when she saw Kathleen, who sprung up from her seat as Wendy and Rita came into the little room.

Kathleen was dressed a little more casually this time, in trousers and a long mohair sweater with complicated designs on it. She was smoking – her third cigarette, judging by the ashtray. When she saw Rita, she seemed to freeze; the cigarette burned unnoticed in her hand.

'Rita! What on earth – what have you done to your hair?'

Rita shrugged. 'I decided you were right. I needed a hair cut. So I got one.'

'But I didn't mean you to – it's a skinhead cut, Rita. I suggested a perm, something feminine . . . '

'Don't you like it then?' asked Rita coolly.

'No. Well, not completely. I mean, yes . . . it takes a bit of getting used to. Yes, I suppose it's all the rage nowadays, isn't it?' Kathleen looked appraisingly at Rita's head and face. 'Actually, it suits you.' She sounded dazed. 'Has Mum seen it?'

'Not yet. Do you think it will give her another stroke?'

Kathleen did not appreciate this attempt at a joke. She looked quite shocked, and there was a stung silence. Then she tried again. 'Perhaps you should have your ears pierced, Rita. Now that your face is on show, some pretty earrings would frame it beautifully.'

She couldn't give it a rest, could she? Kathleen was still trying to turn Rita into a little Barbie doll.

'You're right,' said Rita. 'I was just thinking that myself. I'm going to have two holes in my right ear, and just a small silver stud in my nose. That's the complete look, you know.'

Rita's eyes travelled past Kathleen's splutter of horror and caught Wendy's. The social worker was trying not to laugh, and when she caught Rita's eye she looked quickly away.

'Thanks for the advice about my hair and clothes and stuff,' continued Rita. 'And thanks for the sweatshirt.' She could not bring herself to mention the other clothes Kathleen had bought for her – she would be too tempted to tell Kathleen that they were headed straight for the Oxfam shop.

'You're welcome,' said Kathleen. She shuffled her feet. All three of them were standing, as if sinking into the soft armchairs provided would be an indication that something warm could develop between them. Rita wanted this to be over as quickly as possible. Perhaps Kathleen did, too.

As if she had heard the thought, Kathleen looked

at her watch. 'The train,' she said. 'I'll have to go soon. I just couldn't leave without saying goodbye.'

Rita raised a sceptical eyebrow. 'So Wendy told me,' she said.

Kathleen blushed. 'Look, Rita, I haven't been the best mum in the world, I know that.'

'You weren't the worst either,' said Rita. 'You simply weren't any kind of mother at all.'

It hadn't meant to be as cruel as it sounded, but once the words were out Rita knew that she couldn't call them back. In any case, that was exactly how she felt.

'Oh Rita, how could you?' Kathleen started to cry, and fumbled in her bag. Wendy handed her a tissue. Rita watched Kathleen dabbing carefully at the corners of her eyes. Even in her hour of grief, thought Rita, she can still remember her make up. She suppressed a smile.

'I'm sorry if the truth hurts,' she said coldly. 'But you walk back into my life as if you think I've been waiting for you, like an overdue bus. I'm supposed to fling my arms round you and forgive and forget. Well I can't.'

'No,' said Kathleen in a sudden flash of anger. 'Your gran's seen to that, hasn't she? You've learned how to bear a grudge, Rita. You've learned that from her, the poisonous old witch.'

'Don't talk about my gran like that!' shouted Rita. The careful, cold shield she had built between her and Kathleen dropped. Oh, she wanted to hurt this woman, watch her bleed. If she had a knife in her hand she would use it, she would. Words would have to do – she searched for the most painful ones.

'My gran is the only mother I've ever known.

150

You were just a shadow. You hovered over me at night, stopping me from getting to sleep. I tried to imagine how it would be if you came back. Sometimes I thought I would like it, but now I've seen you I'm glad you stayed away all those years. Yes, I'm glad. Gran and me have been happier than we could ever have been with you.'

'Rita, calm down,' said Wendy uneasily. 'I don't think you're giving Kathleen a fair chance to explain – '

'Explain? That would be interesting,' said Rita bitterly. 'No, actually it *would* have been interesting, years ago when I was wondering why she never telephoned, never wrote, never even made sure I knew she was alive. But I'm not interested now. I just want her to go.'

Kathleen rose to her feet, smoothing her clothes and picking up her bag. The tears had dried, and there were two red angry patches burning on her cheeks. 'You think it's so easy,' she said. 'I hope you're never standing in my shoes, Rita. I hope you never live to hear your own daughter treating you like dirt.'

Rita had run out of steam. She felt tired, she wanted this to be over. She turned away from Kathleen and walked over to the window. 'You always had a choice,' she said over her shoulder. 'And I'll never be in your shoes. If I had a child, not heaven and not earth would keep me away from her.'

Kathleen sobbed. She was crying again. Rita turned to look at her, perhaps for the last time. Wendy was looking very sadly at Kathleen, not wanting to intervene but clearly feeling very sorry for her. Tears were running down Kathleen's cheeks now, her make-up apparently forgotten. The tissue was clutched in Kathleen's hand, soggy, daubed with black smudges.

Rita watched this woman, her mother, crying and wondered if there was something wrong inside her that she didn't feel compassion. She felt only a sense of justice. Kathleen deserved to feel bad, and tears didn't hurt enough. But with the justice came a bit of mercy, not for Kathleen's sake but for Rita's.

In years to come you'll remember this and you'll feel guilty, thought Rita. You won't remember how she deserved it, you'll only remember how horrible you were. For this reason, Rita realized she should be merciful – not to spare her mother the pain, but to spare herself the guilt of causing the suffering.

'I didn't mean all of that. I didn't mean it to sound as horrible as that,' she said lamely. 'The thing is, I never knew anything about you. Gran never talked, I never asked. And now it just feels like it's too late to start over again. We're different people, we don't know anything about each other. I don't want you to go telling your husband about me, risking your marriage and all that, to try and build something out of nothing. I'm glad you came, but I don't think it's a good idea to drag this out. Let's just get on with our own lives, eh? No hard feelings, just – well, just leaving each other alone. Can we?'

Rita felt herself very close to tears as Kathleen turned away from her, obviously trying to regain her composure. Her shoulders shook, and Wendy looked as if she would move to put an arm around the woman, but Kathleen gained control and turned back to face Rita.

'You're right,' she said. 'Your gran's done a good job on you, Rita. I wish you well, I really do. Tell you what, I'll come and dance at your wedding, eh? You just let me know when you need me. I'll be there.'

Not on your nelly, thought Rita. It was one of Gran's sayings. Not on your nelly, she repeated to herself, and it gave her the strength to say out loud, 'Yes, p'raps.'

'God, look at the time. I'm sorry – I've got to go, really I have. 'Bye, Rita.'

There was a hug, and a kiss. It was hurried, and nervous, like a soft, fluttering bird moving past Rita's cheek. It was the only moment when Rita's mother came close enough for Rita to smell her: perfume, cigarette smoke and warmth. She breathed in slowly and closed her eyes. When she opened them the door was swinging slowly shut. Her mother was gone.

'You OK?' said Wendy anxiously. There were tears in her eyes. Rita grinned, and offered her a hanky. 'Yes, I think so. We'd better go and see Gran now, before I chicken out.'

Gran's reaction to Rita's hair was predictable: first a look of disbelief, then anger and a low growling sound as Gran tried to form words which would properly express her outrage. Her face, already twisted by the effects of the stroke, had the look of an evil cartoon witch, and although Gran couldn't say much it was clear enough to leave Rita feeling very bad indeed.

'I'm sorry, Gran. It was just so difficult to look

after properly, I got fed up with it and decided to go for a completely new look. I went over the top, I know. But it'll soon grow.'

Gran stared and stared at her, but said nothing. Rita could almost read the whirlwind of angry thoughts that whizzed around her grandmother's brain, and saw the frustration of someone so used to speaking her mind being imprisoned by the difficulty of actually getting the words together in a sensible order. That made her feel even worse. She apologized again and again. Gran, seeing how upset she was, finally sighed and settled back on her pillow, waving a dismissive hand. 'Sooner we're home, the better,' she said finally. And that was it.

Wendy discussed with Gran the arrangements for getting help at home when the old lady left hospital. Rita could see her gran struggling to follow it all, and becoming confused sometimes. Rita took Gran's hand. 'Don't worry, Gran. I'll be able to look after you. Wendy's going to try and get us some home help, and there's the neighbours. Everybody's missing you, Gran. Just get well, and get out of here. I want to come home, with you.'

'That's certainly our plan,' said Wendy. 'Of course, Mrs Dennison, we will have to talk very carefully about how you're going to manage . . .'
Rita started to daydream. The flat would be warm; there would be flowers from Mrs Nelson's window-box, and a fruit cake from Miss Smith. The tea would be brewed and the fire stoked in the parlour. Maybe things would never be quite the same, but they would be familiar and they would be Rita's own. She pictured Gran sitting in her chair, holding forth about the government's latest 'foolhardiness'

as Gran liked to put it, with her friends arguing and waving their tea cups at each other. Those arguments had bored her in the past; now she felt homesick for them.

'Kathleen gone?' she heard Gran asking, and realized the question was directed at her. Gran's eyes were bright, and she was trying to read Rita's thoughts about Kathleen. Rita could see all the unanswered questions about how she and Kathleen had got along, what Rita thought of her, and how she felt about Gran keeping Kathleen a secret. But although she felt sorry for Gran and could understand why she had done what she did, Rita did not feel Gran deserved easy answers. She was not ready to share how she felt about it all. She didn't even know herself properly yet.

'Yes, she's gone. She said she'd be in touch.' That was all Gran could have.

Gran closed her eyes. She was so tired with the effort of trying to take in what was going on around her. Rita stroked her hand. Wendy said softly that she would leave the two of them alone for a while, and come back later to give Rita a lift back to the Browns.

When Wendy had gone, Gran opened her eyes. Rita had the feeling that she had only been pretending to be asleep.

'There'll be none of this silliness when we're both home,' Gran said suddenly, her mouth trying to twist round the words. 'Your lovely long hair . . . how could you!'

'Actually,' said Rita calmly, 'I've decided to keep it short – not like this, but definitely not long. I *like* short hair.'

Gran snorted in disgust. 'Look like a boy,' she said.

'That's very sexist, Gran,' said Rita calmly. 'Anyway, I don't see how you can say that. How many times have I heard you complain about all the boys growing their hair long. I do believe your exact words were, "There'll be no real men left at this rate." '

Gran chuckled. There was something different about Rita today. She had always been a shy, pale little thing. Now she looked stronger, more confident. 'Rita, you are growing up,' she said.

Rita took her gran's outstretched hand. 'I certainly am,' she said.